SARAH M. ANDERSON WRITING AS

MAGGIE CHASE

THEIR
EMERALD

Acknowledgements

I could not have written this book without the generous help of the following people: Melissa Jolly for everything she does, Shae O'Conner and Laura K. Curtis for their support, Tasha Harrison and Mary Dieterich for editing, and Alexandra Haughton for designing the cover.

Dedication

To Victoria Dahl

Chapter One

1867

H e was late.

Emmy wondered if she could check the calendar without being obvious about it. It was Tuesday, wasn't it? And Tuesday was Raymond's night. He had been paying a call to her here at the Jeweled Ladies every Tuesday for the last eight months. He paid Mistress an exorbitant amount of money to procure Emmy's services for the entire night.

He didn't like to share, he said out loud. She was the only woman for him, he told anyone who would listen. The entire town of Brimstone—and perhaps all of Texas—knew it. Mayor Raymond Dupree may keep company with a whore like Emerald Green, but he was so steadfast and devoted some people didn't count that as a mark against him.

The clock on the mantel chimed six thirty. It was fine painted porcelain, with delicate paste jewels of blue and green embedded into the pattern over its long sloping shoulders. Ladylike, Mistress insisted. Everything inside the Jeweled Ladies brothel was ladylike.

And, just like the paste jewels, nearly everything here was a fake, a trick of the eye. But wasn't that what men wanted? They didn't want something real.

1

They paid for the lie and the more convincing the lie, the more they paid.

Emerald Green was the highest paid lady here.

And right now, she was fretting. It wasn't like Raymond to be late. They had a standing appointment. Over the months, Emmy had come to treasure her Tuesday evenings. For once a week, she didn't have to be Emerald Green, the second most famous whore in Brimstone, Texas. Mistress was, of course, the most famous and Emmy was her protégé. The Jeweled Ladies would be hers one day—if no one made an honest woman out of her before that.

She doubted that would happen. Raymond's affections for her were widely known yet he, sadly, was not the marrying kind.

Mistress swept into the parlor, a confection of pink silk and perfect makeup. The original Jeweled Lady was well into her fortieth year—rumored to be closer to fifty—but with pink shades on the lights, she could still pass for her early thirties. Younger, if the brandy snifter has been emptied.

Mistress's eyes swept the parlor and landed upon Emmy. Emmy straightened under her gaze. Mistress was, by all standards, a fair and kind employer. Emmy knew better than anyone that not all madams cared for their girls. Mistress did—in her own way.

Mistress did not so much make a beeline for Emmy, but her destination was unmistakable. The parlor was the formal room at the brothel and everyone in it was required to act accordingly. None of the girls were allowed into the parlor with their hair down or without a gown. Absolutely nothing untoward occurred in the parlor.

2

However, the saloon across the hall was a different story. There, Mistress would allow certain girls to come down in nothing but their petticoats and corsets, their bosoms temptingly on display. Along one whole wall of the saloon ran a hand-carved walnut bar manned by Sterling Silver, a handsome youth who would discreetly take coin from a discerning ladies and gentleman for a private nightcap.

A small stage stood at one end of the saloon, where girls with talent could sing and dance—and disrobe, if the price was right. Card games often broke out, but Samuel, Mistress's black doorman, made sure there was no fighting. Men who were looking to brawl found themselves bodily thrown out of the Jeweled Ladies and forbidden from returning—ever.

The Jeweled Ladies was not a whorehouse, but the finest brothel this side of the Mississippi and Mistress enforced this distinction ruthlessly.

As Mistress worked her way toward Emmy, she stopped and spoke to each of the couples in the parlor. Garnet was taking tea with a young farmer Emmy had never seen before. The young man couldn't have been more than eighteen and his jittery hands gave away his nervousness. Garnet would take care of him, though. Virgins were her specialty.

Pearl was at the piano, as she usually was at this time of the evening. The girl had been trained out East. She had three gentlemen around her, each staring at her with moony eyes—but would any of them pay to have Pearl be cruel to them? Needless to say, men who saw Pearl did not bother with Emmy, thank goodness.

Ebony was not long for this parlor—anyone could see that she and her gentleman caller, Roy Griffin, the proprietor of the Golden Star hotel, would soon have to vacate this room, lest they violate Mistress's parlor rules.

Ebony was another example of Mistress's fairness. She was a former slave. Women like Ebony often wound up in the worst whorehouses, but Mistress had happily taken on the girl. There had been an adjustment period, of course. Not all of the girls were comfortable with Ebony—although they didn't mind Samuel. But then, Samuel didn't hold the same position in the Jeweled Ladies as the girls—and several had been loath to admit a colored girl into their rarified ranks.

Mistress had informed them all that Ebony was staying and if they didn't like it, they were more than welcome to seek employment elsewhere.

No one had left. All of the girls knew that the Jeweled Ladies was the rare place where they could be treated as queens and paid accordingly. And Emerald Green had learned another lesson about managing a house full of whores. Wealth was power but loyalty? Loyalty trumped all.

Personally, Emmy found Ebony to be sweet and charming—and Ebony could sew the most wonderful dresses and corsets, seemingly out of nothing. That's what had finally won the others over. No whore worth her salt would turn down a dress—especially not in this part of Texas, where high fashion was at least twenty years out of date.

Mistress smiled at Ebony. That was all it took to remind the girl of the rules. By the time Mistress made it to her destination, Ebony and Roy had excused themselves from the room.

"He's late," Mistress said with no other introduction. She smiled prettily but her voice was low and worried. "Have you heard from him? It's not like him to miss his night."

Emmy swallowed down her nerves. Raymond was a fair mayor—but he still had his enemies. Brimstone could be a rough town, as was this entire part of Texas, swelling daily with an influx of veterans of the Civil War and former slaves, all looking for work on the massive cattle drives.

One of the things Raymond had done as mayor was to enact restrictions on private guns inside the city limits in an attempt to clean up the town. This restriction had made him enemies more than anything else, but there were too many murders when Yankees and Rebels got to drinking in the saloons. The war had been over for two years now. Raymond had won his election by promising that, by 1868, Brimstone would be a respectable town.

Emmy didn't know where the Jeweled Ladies fit into this new, respectable future. They were as respectable as whores could be—but whores all the same. "I'm sure he'll be here."

For a moment, Mistress looked sympathetic—but the moment was short. She patted Emmy on the arm and said, "I've had an inquiry. If he doesn't show…"

Emmy made sure to school her features into pleasant blankness. "Oh? Who?"

The lines around Mistress's eyes tightened. "We shall cross that bridge when we get to it, dear."

She looked nervous, Emmy realized. And that terrified Emmy. Because Mistress knew how to handle men and handle them well. If someone could make Mistress nervous, then what could they do to Emmy?

"I will not be tied and whipped," she said in a

voice that barely qualified as a whisper. "I will *not*. Send him to Sapphire." Sapphire was the girl who didn't just tolerate being whipped—she actually liked it. Needed it, she'd told Emmy once.

Emmy hadn't understood then and she didn't understand now—nor did she understand how men needed Pearl to do the same to them. But she'd been whoring long enough to know that different people needed different things in the bedroom and so, if Sapphire needed someone to bind her wrists, it only made sense that there were men out there who needed to bind her.

But that would not be Emmy. Not again. Never again.

Mistress smiled as if, no, of course the inquiry hadn't involved *that*. But Emmy saw the woman swallow. "He asked for you specifically."

To anyone else in the room, it looked as if Emmy and Mistress were just having a pleasant conversation, perhaps about the weather. But Emmy was seething. "I follow your rules, Mistress. You follow mine. That is the deal."

It had always been the deal. Mistress took in girls who had potential, intelligence and beauty and she trained them to be the finest of whores. It didn't matter their race—Mistress treated them all as equals. Each girl worked for as long as she wanted and then she could move on, usually with a fat bank account to support her. They had had men from London, even from Paris, in their parlor who'd said that the Jeweled Ladies were just as fine as the ladies of the night in Europe, if not better. It was a source of pride for Mistress.

The girls had to follow the rules. They gave up their names and became Jewels. They spent money on clothes and learned how to act in the parlor, how to please in the bedroom. They did what Mistress said, wore what she told them to wear, acted as she did. And in return, Mistress paid them handsomely and made sure that a girl never did anything with anyone she didn't want to. The Jewels were not just highly trained and polished to a shine. They had a say in who they spread their legs for. Mistress never forced them.

Until, it seemed, now. "You would be handsomely rewarded," she coaxed. "A hundred dollars, if not more."

Emmy's stomach turned. That kind of money was nothing to joke about—but she couldn't sell her sanity for a mere hundred dollars. If Mistress sold her time to someone who wanted to watch her beg, Emmy would... well, she would leave. It would be a blow to her plans, that much was for sure. But she had almost twenty-five hundred dollars saved in the First Macon County Bank—more than enough to start over. She'd be giving up the Jeweled Ladies and a lifetime of financial security but for Mistress to go back against her word like that would be a violation that could *not* be repaired.

Being a whore was not always bad. In fact, Emmy occasionally enjoyed large parts of it. Being the second most famous whore in Brimstone meant that she could command a higher price—which meant better clientele. She had a few regulars whom she liked being with and the rest was... Well, it wasn't worth the trouble it took to think over it.

Still, Tuesdays were her very favorite evening of the week because everyone else paid for a night with Emerald Green. Only Raymond paid for Emmy.

She knew she could go to Raymond and he would take her in. But a whore fleeing her madam could very well destroy his career. No, she couldn't do that to Raymond. She cared for him far too much.

There was another option, if she had to leave quickly. Free Cyrus Franklin was rumored to take in runaways and former slaves and help them on their way West. He'd helped Millie, who—briefly—had been Miss Topaz Gold before she'd disappeared. Maybe Franklin would be able to spirit her away and protect her until she could get her money and come up with a new plan.

Mistress smiled—but it didn't reach her eyes. "I'm sure he'll be here," she said, patting Emmy on the arm. "Let us not fret over something that most likely won't come to pass."

Fret? This was not fretting. This was white-hot rage burning on a pyre of fear. "*Mistress*—"

The bell over the front door jingled and both women paused, their ears cocked toward the entrance. "Mayor Dupree," Samuel's deep voice rumbled. "Let me help you with your coat, sir."

Emmy exhaled in relief.

Mistress patted Emmy on the arm again and smiled. Even with her polish and her makeup, Emmy thought she looked visibly thankful. "Excellent. Have a lovely evening, dear."

It took real effort to school her face into blandness, but Emmy had been trained by the very best. "And you as well, Mistress. I shall see you tomorrow."

Mistress sashayed off to greet Raymond. Samuel was the first line of defense for the Jeweled Ladies. But Mistress had the final say on who was allowed to patronize her establishment. As such, she preferred to be on a first name basis with each and every one of her customers. They were all friends here, she liked to say.

If only Mistress knew. Emmy turned from her window just as Raymond entered the parlor, that mischievous smile on his face. Oh, good. His spirits were high and he looked whole. She should not have worried. "Raymond," she said, putting a note of severity into her voice.

Unlike Mistress's meandering path to her, Raymond did not stop to exchange pleasantries with anyone else in the parlor. He made straight for her and, grasping her offered hand in his, he bowed low over it before pressing his lips to her knuckles. "I do hope you can forgive me, Miss Green. My tardiness is nearly unforgivable. I can only pray that you will not hold it against me this evening."

When she met his gaze, she saw that his eyes were unusually bright. She supposed that, to the outside observer, they looked like they did every Tuesday. But she could tell something had happened— and it was something good. "Shall we?" Which was a slight breach of their protocol. Normally, they shared a drop of sherry before they adjourned to her room. But they had already lost a half an hour and she was in no mood to wait to find out what had him so jubilant. Right now, she needed the comfort he provided.

Raymond stood and tucked her hand into the corner of his elbow. His gaze never left hers as they strolled out of the parlor and took the wide staircase that led up to the second floor. Emmy was the center of his world right now. Her only regret about her arrangement with Raymond was that there would never be anything more than this.

9

They did not speak until her bedroom door was shut firmly behind them and she had shot the lock. She stepped into Raymond and began loosening his necktie. "What has happened?"

"My darling Emmy, it is the most extraordinary thing." She undid the buttons of his waistcoat and shirt and then she turned so that he could work at the buttons at the back of her gown. They did this every Tuesday, undressing each other like an old married couple until he was in nothing but his drawers and she in her shift. As he unlaced her corset, she exhaled in satisfaction. Oh, how she loved Tuesdays.

"Tell me," she insisted. "Do not leave me hanging on your every word."

He held her hand as she stepped out of her gown and then picked it up and shook it out for her, draping it over the top of her dressing screen. He was so thoughtful like that. "You won't believe it. I scarcely believe it myself."

Emmy moved to the bed and pulled down the covers. "Raymond, you are teasing me. What's happened? I was worried about you when you didn't show." She left out the part where she'd been worried Mistress was going to break her word. She didn't want to distract Raymond from his happiness.

She slid into bed and held the covers for him. He climbed in after her and tucked his arm around her shoulder. She curled into his warm, broad chest but she did not rest her head upon him. Instead, she propped herself up and stared down at him. "Out with it."

His smile—*oh*. It must be very good. He brushed a curl away from her forehead and said, "He kissed me."

Shock stilled her hand from ruffling the scattering

of hair upon his chest. Those three words had just changed her world. "Hank?"

"Hank," Raymond repeated, glowing with happiness.

"But I thought you said... He wasn't... Are you *sure*?" Because she had been sure. Raymond had been sure until today, apparently.

She loved Raymond. Raymond loved her. But his heart belonged to Hank O'Shea and Hank did not love Raymond. Not like *that*.

"I didn't think he was," Raymond mused.

Conflicting emotions washed through her. She ducked her head down to hide her confusion. Automatically, his hand came up and he began to stroke her hair and her shoulder. "How did it happen?" she asked, putting extra effort into keeping her voice light and happy.

She hated pretending because that was the one thing that she didn't have to do with Raymond. In the safety of this room, together they could be who they really were and she didn't want that to change.

But she wasn't sure she could be happy for him because if Hank O'Shea fell in love with Raymond the way Raymond already loved Hank, where would she be?

Alone. That wasn't entirely true because she would remain here, her services in high demand and her future assured as the handpicked successor to Mistress. But she would no longer be Raymond's confidant, his closest friend. She would no longer be his Emmy and that thought saddened her far more than she wanted to.

"He brought me paperwork to sign," Raymond said, still sounding as if he did not believe his good fortune. "He leaned over the desk to arrange the papers for me and..." He shrugged. "I didn't lean back. I asked a question and he turned his face toward me and I almost kissed him then and there, but I was afraid."

Emmy nodded against his chest. Raymond was rightfully terrified of being found out. Even as he was trying to make Brimstone more genteel, it was still a rough town and people who stepped outside of the rules dictated by society were punished swiftly and mercilessly. Emmy may have started out as a shield against the fate that awaited men like Raymond but she had thought that she had become much more than that.

"And he was as close to me as I am to you—except that we weren't touching." She could see it in her mind's eye, Raymond sitting in his office chair in his office and Hank O'Shea practically draped across his lap on the desk. It was a pose that she would've used to entice a man. Begrudgingly, she admired Hank's approach.

"What did he say?" Because she wanted all the details. She would not panic about this change until she knew for sure whether or not it would affect her.

She and Raymond had never shared more than this—kisses on the hand and forehead, long talks in bed. It was a different sort of intimacy than she was used to sharing with the men who paid for her time, and in many ways it was far more revealing than simply taking off her clothes and spreading her legs would ever be.

She didn't want to lose this.

She was being selfish. Raymond was not here for her. She was here for Raymond. He was her best customer and also her closest friend and she needed to work harder on being happy for him.

"He leaned in closer and he said, 'Is that really what you want to know?' And he held me with his gaze and..." Raymond's voice trailed off and, perhaps unconsciously, he held her tighter at the memory of holding someone else. "And I said no. That wasn't the question I meant to ask."

"What did he do next?" She had to admit, it all sounded romantic. She was happy for Raymond, she decided. One of the many things he shared with her over their time together was that he despaired of ever finding anyone who would accept him as he was— anyone besides her, that was.

"He said, 'I didn't think so.' And then he kissed me." He sighed, a noise of bone-deep contentment.

He didn't say anything else, but Emmy didn't need him to. She could picture it all. Lips and tongues and hands everywhere as Raymond first held himself back and then, under the assault of Hank's mouth, gave himself over to pleasure. Perhaps the first true pleasure he'd ever known. "Was it good?" she asked—not to torture herself, but because she really did want her friend to be happy.

He shuddered, a ripple of satisfaction that moved through his entire body. The bedclothes peaked around his midsection. He had never been so aroused in her bed before. "It was... *amazing*," he sighed. "Better than I ever dreamed."

And although she was worried about what this meant for her and him and their friendship, she smiled because no matter how much she loved Raymond, she could never bring him this happiness. "And?" Because of her experience, nothing that started with a kiss ever ended with one.

13

"And… And when it was over," he said going on in an attempt at seriousness, "he leaned back and asked if that was the answer I was looking for. And I said yes." He looked at her and cupped her face in his palms. "This changes things, you know."

"I know," she sighed. "But I am so happy for you, Raymond." For that was something she had learned long ago, to be happy for her customers and to keep her sadness for herself inside.

They snuggled together under the covers, talking about their days but studiously avoiding any talk of the future.

She would just have to do what she always did when things changed. She would hold her head up high and glide through life, not letting it touch her.

But this, she thought, would be harder than ever before.

Chapter Two

Raymond's hands shook as he strode toward City Hall the next morning. For so long, it seemed like nothing would ever change. He would always be stuck in the purgatory of loneliness, wanting what he could not allow himself to have. And yet, within the last day, *everything* had changed so suddenly and so completely that he wasn't quite sure what was going to happen next.

Well, he *knew* what was going to happen in the immediate future. He was going to walk into his office and pretend like the kiss that happened yesterday hadn't. Because he still wasn't convinced that it had been real. He had fantasized about kissing Hank O'Shea for so long that it was entirely possible that it was a figment of his imagination.

But then, if he'd imagined it, it wouldn't have stopped with the kiss.

What if it had been some sort of trap laid for him by his political opponents? This was the thought that haunted him, because he had enemies as he tried to drag Brimstone toward the civility of the 1870s. There were certain groups that didn't like his ban on firearms inside the city limits. The saloon owners were behind him, but their customers weren't. The cattle ranchers were against his bringing the railroad through town, carving up their grazing lands and risking their cattle. The Comanche were a problem that required constant vigilance.

But more than those problems, there were plenty of people who simply didn't like Raymond because they still hated his father, Leopold Dupree—including Judge Gerard Hobson, who'd been building his political base ever since Leopold had drowned with Raymond's mother, Isabelle, in a rare flash flood years ago. Judge Hobson had made it clear—Raymond was nothing but his father's name and Hobson would do everything in his power to destroy Raymond.

Raymond was not about to let that happen. But the man was hell-bent on trying. And one of the issues that the two of them clashed over was Free Cyrus Franklin, the black man who owned land outside of Brimstone and who took in former slaves and runaways, giving them a hand up as they journeyed out West to find a new beginning.

Personally, Raymond admired what Franklin did. He understood the unfairness of people treating a person differently because of something that couldn't be helped. It wasn't quite the same, because of course Raymond was an affluent, landowning white man— and the mayor at that. All he had to do was pretend that he spent his Tuesday evenings making vigorous love to Emerald Green, the most beautiful woman in Brimstone. His life would be much harder if his truth was something he couldn't hide.

So, yes, he supported Free Franklin but politically, there were enough people in town that didn't approve of a black man helping out other black men and women—because apparently they believed it encouraged other colored people to come to town and those morally corrupt bigots simply couldn't have *that*.

And the man who voiced that disapproval the loudest was none other than Judge Gerard Hobson. He couched it in terms of lawful behavior—Free Franklin was most likely skirting some sort of law or another—but the dislike bordered on hatred.

Hobson would do anything, it seemed, to undermine Raymond. *Anything*.

This was the thought that kept him up long after he had left the Jeweled Ladies last night. What if Hank kissing him hadn't been what Raymond desperately wanted it to be? Raymond's grand political plans—a run at the statehouse, and then the governorship of Texas—all hung in the balance of that kiss being real and honest and true.

Because it wouldn't just be his political plans ruined, should Hank make claims about Raymond in public. Raymond would be run out of town and, indeed, out of Texas. His life would be in danger and, no matter where he went, there would always be a risk that whispers would work their way to new ears.

If Hank's kiss had been false, Raymond would have to get married. It would be the only way to preserve his reputation. But it was also the surest way to madness.

If only he could marry Emmy. It wouldn't be such a bad life. She knew who he was and she understood him in a way that no one else ever had. She could take discreet lovers and he could as well and they could both come to bed in the evening and talk of their days.

But marrying a whore—even one as cultivated and

17

refined as Emerald Green—was not a smart political move. Which meant, that if he had to, Raymond would be forced to marry someone like Cynthia Hobbs, the banker's daughter. And then he would be forced to pretend that he desired her. He would have to make love to her and do so in a way that convinced her—and the world—he loved her. He wouldn't mind children and a family—but the thought of having to live a lie for the rest of his life sickened him.

Unable to deal with that thought, Raymond's mind turned back to Hank. It was a wise thing to do, to prepare for the worst. But he couldn't bear the thought of Hank betraying him any more than he could bear the thought of the kiss having been a trap. Hank had been his man of business for the last eighteen months. He had been a combination campaign manager, personal secretary and enforcer, when the need arose. Brimstone was a town that was trying to shed its rough past—but there were still edges that were rough and Raymond needed someone who didn't mind getting a little blood on his knuckles.

And Hank had such lovely knuckles. The whole of his hands were the stuff of fantasies. Hank O'Shea was a solid six foot two of muscle and rough brawn. As Raymond understood it, Hank had brawled his way from Ireland to the shores of America, although he didn't know anything more than that. Somewhere on the East Coast—Hank wouldn't say where—he had picked up some education and then decided to move farther West, to better his chances of bettering himself. He had arrived in Brimstone two years ago. Raymond had hired him a mere two months after that. Since that moment, Raymond had thought of little else.

18

He ran through the advice that Emmy had given him last night—he trusted her completely. Raymond was to go in to City Hall this morning as if nothing had happened. He was not even to look longingly in Hank's direction. He was not to say anything out of the ordinary. Everything must be exactly the same as it ever was, so that no one would remark upon the difference.

Then, after whatever business Raymond needed to accomplish had been finished, he was to call Hank into his office for a private meeting. Emmy had recommended letting Hank make the first move. She said that if Hank crossed the line between the visitor's side of Raymond's desk and came to where Raymond sat a second time, then the sign would be unmistakable. But, sadly, she had been unable to tell Raymond what proof he needed that would demonstrate Hank's sincerity and attraction, or what would happen after that. Emmy knew a great deal about the ways of men—but there were limits and this was one of them.

Nothing had happened. This was what Raymond told himself. One of the things that made him an excellent politician was his ability to sincerely believe what he was telling his constituents—a skill he had long perfected by convincing people that he sincerely enjoyed women. Therefore, Hank had not kissed him and Raymond had not kissed him back. It was that simple.

Resolved, he opened the door and walked in to City Hall. Hank was behind his desk and stood immediately and Raymond realized that nothing would ever be simple ever again because even just seeing the man, his suit jacket straining at the shoulders and his blue eyes twinkling with an emotion that Raymond hoped was anticipation nearly destroyed him. "Good morning, Mr. O'Shea."

One of Hank's eyebrows twitched up momentarily, but immediately his face was impassive. He was not the most expressive man. "Morning, Mayor Dupree," he said, his Irish accent lilting at the ends. "How was your evening with Miss Green?"

This was a perfectly normal conversation for them on Wednesday morning. But it didn't feel normal. Did Hank wonder if Raymond had left their kiss in the office and transferred his passion to Emmy? Or did he suspect now that Emmy was nothing but a shield?

Please let it be real. "Miss Green was a delight, as always," he said calmly. Even though she was a whore, Raymond's steadfast devotion to her reflected well on him.

"Shall I order the usual flowers?" This is another part of their normal routine. Raymond always sent a gift to Emmy on Wednesday. During the summer season, it was flowers. At times, he had had fine chocolates brought in from Houston. For special occasions, such as her birthday, he had ordered expensive French perfume and fine lavender soaps all the way from England.

But something occurred to him as he looked at Hank while trying not to stare in open adoration. Emmy had been thrilled for him, of course—but Raymond had an itching feeling that there had been something that bothered her about this new development. Perhaps she was concerned that her position would be affected? Or was she more worried about Hank's motives? No, Raymond decided, it couldn't be that. If she were concerned about Hank's motives, she would've said as much. She was loyal and protective of him and for that—among other reasons— he loved her dearly.

"Send the flowers," he decided. "But I need to get her something special. A necklace, perhaps." Emmys décolletage was a thing to be admired and a diamond pendant would set it off to its best advantage.

The corner of Hank's mouth twitched up. It wasn't a big, wide smile—but then again, Hank was not a big, expressive man. It was a small, intimate smile meant only for Raymond. It made his blood pound. "So it was a very good night, then?"

Raymond swallowed. "One of the better evenings of my life," he said honestly.

The other corner of Hank's mouth twitched up—a blink-and-you-missed-it grin. Raymond hadn't missed it. "I am delighted to hear that, sir. There are a few things that I would like to discuss with you—in private."

Raymond's heart leapt with joy. But before he could say anything else, Hank went on, "However, you have several meetings this morning and Mr. Hobbs is already in your office. He claims it is urgent."

Raymond rolled his eyes and Hank nodded. *Everything* was urgent to Gene Hobbs. He ran the First Macon County Bank and, because of that, he was operating under the illusion that he also ran the town. It was a constant battle for Raymond to dissuade him of this notion. "Very well. We shall speak later?"

It was not exactly what Emmy had told him to do. The conversation had strayed slightly from the norm— but not so far that it would set off any warning bells to anyone who'd overheard it. Including Mr. Hobbs, who was no doubt listening.

Hank's gaze caressed Raymond's face. "I shall look forward to it."

It was wrong and a sin and Raymond was undoubtedly going to go to hell. But he wanted Hank O'Shea and for the first time, it seemed as if he might actually get what he wanted.

Chapter Three

The workday passed slowly without a chance for Hank to speak with Raymond in private. Raymond was a busy man. In addition to his scheduled meetings, Sheriff Cutler invited him to lunch to discuss the ban on weapons inside city limits and of course Raymond had to accept. After lunch there was a meeting with a concerned group of citizens from the Baptist Church about Free Cyrus Franklin and, after the school day had ended, the prim schoolmistress Miss Minerva Krenshaw presented herself to demand more money for her pupils' education. From the tone of her voice this time, it sounded like she wanted new books.

Every single time someone left Raymond's office, Hank waited to see if this would be a break. He needed to see if he had lost his job or if there was something else Raymond wanted out of him. Something that involved fewer meetings and vastly less clothing.

It was the *something else* that kept his mind drifting. In addition to scheduling meetings with interested parties and constituents, Hank was responsible for managing Raymond Dupree's political future. Earlier this year, there had been a call for a new constitution for the state of Texas and, if Hank did his job right, Raymond would be a delegate when the

23

convention met. From there, it would be easy to win a seat in the state legislature. Raymond would hold several terms, and then he would make a run for governor. The man was brilliant and he knew how to talk to people.

Hank had seen from the very beginning that Raymond Dupree was a man who was going places— places that Hank would never get on his own. No one wanted to give power to a Black Irish orphan. But he could help someone else take power. Politics, like life, was a dirty business and Hank had no problem getting a little mud on his hands.

But it was difficult to focus on these goals when his mind kept turning back to last night. He still didn't know what had come over him. He had not actually meant to kiss Raymond.

For months, he had suspected that Raymond held him in a different affection than he might afford another employee. Raymond Dupree had a way of looking at Hank through hooded eyes that any man would notice. And, after months of careful observation, Hank had in fact concluded that Raymond didn't look at anyone else like that. Man *or* woman. Those intense, longing stares were for Hank and Hank alone.

But Raymond had never made a move and Hank had begun to wonder if he knew how. Part of Hank's new start out West was giving up men. And women. He was going to be a man of quality, not a street rat taking comfort where comfort was offered—for whatever price was offered.

Hank had been celibate for three years now. He had his fair share of offers from lovely women who were looking for a little entertainment on the side while their husbands ignored them—but he hadn't taken anyone up on those offers because that's not who he was anymore. He was a serious man of business. No one would know about the scrawny runt named Henry Moynihan who survived on the streets. That boy was dead to the world and in his place, Hank O'Shea had risen. It hadn't been pretty and often not legal—but he had money in the bank, decent rooms in a boarding house and food in his belly. He had a job. He had a future.

Did he have Raymond?

Yesterday had been a moment of weakness. Celibacy was lonely, it turned out. Hank had convinced himself that, by abstaining, he was redeeming himself for the sins of the past. But Raymond kept watching him with his hooded brown eyes. If that's all there was to it, Hank would have kept his hands and his mouth to himself. But he liked Raymond. For a politician, he was a surprisingly decent human being. He was tough but fair and only occasionally had he used Hank's fists to settle an issue.

Hank had been watching him for months and months now. He wasn't proud of some of the things he had done—staying up all night to watch Raymond's house in order to see if anyone came or left under cover of darkness, tailing him to the Jeweled Ladies to be sure that that was where he spent his Tuesdays, investigating Emerald Green to make sure she couldn't damage Raymond's career. But no one slipped into Raymond Dupree's house under cover of darkness and the only woman he spent time with was Emerald Green.

Hank respected the man. Respect bred admiration

and admiration bred affection. A fierce, protective affection. Raymond was a good-looking man, impeccably dressed in the latest styles that suited his lean frame, a trim moustache over his lip—never a hair out of place on his head.

Yesterday, Raymond had kissed him back. It had been awkward, but exhilarating. Hank didn't want to start over again. But he would, if that's what Raymond decided was best. California was opening up and a man could start fresh and leave his past behind for a third time.

After what felt like an eternity, the schoolmistress stormed out of City Hall. Miss Krenshaw was so mad that she didn't even sneer at Hank—which was new. Raymond must have said no to whatever she'd wanted.

It was close to five o'clock now and nothing else was on the schedule.

Hank was no innocent. He hadn't been since he'd been a child, maybe even before that. But this was something new, even to him, this anticipation. Before he'd come to Brimstone, if there had been something he wanted, he took it. And if there had been something someone wanted of him, they took it, too. Life was about taking—not about waiting.

He was waiting now. Raymond was in his office with the door closed and Hank was waiting for a sign. He wanted to walk in that office and haul Raymond out of his chair and kiss the man until they were both shaking with need—need that would finally, *finally* be answered.

He wouldn't have thought the clock could go any slower, but it did. Seconds stretched for years, minutes took eternities. And still, Raymond did not call him in.

Dammit. He'd screwed this up somehow. It was becoming more clear by the second that Hank did not know how a man of quality engaged in liaisons. He knew how men of quality *paid* for liaisons, but that wasn't what was happening here.

Just when he couldn't take another second, the door opened and there stood Raymond. He had removed his suit jacket and stood in his waistcoat, his cuffs still fastened. Not a hair on his sandy brown head had been mussed, despite the long workday. He was as he ever was—*perfect*.

"Is that it, then?" he asked in a level voice.

Hank stood, his notebook in his hand. He was never nervous, so to be nervous at all was uncharacteristic for him. But he was, anyway. "Aye. Nothing else on the schedule."

The lines around Raymond's eyes deepened and, to Hank, he looked pleased. "Do we have time to discuss plans, or is there somewhere you need to be this evening?"

Hank translated. *Will you come to me or will you leave?* "I'm not expected anywhere else tonight."

A smile graced Raymond's lips. It was faint, but it was there. "Excellent. Do come in."

Hank moved toward the door and Raymond retreated. He went around his desk, but he did not sit in his chair. Instead, he stood, fiddling with his cuffs. Hank closed the door behind him and waited. Patience was not his strong suit and no matter what happened, he did not want to hurt Raymond.

He would prefer not to be hurt himself, but he could take the pain. He had survived worse.

The moment stretched. Apparently, Raymond was

waiting for him to take the lead—but he was waiting for Raymond to do the same. Well, then. Hank swallowed and did what he always did—jumped in with both feet. "About last night…"

Raymond tensed and Hank hesitated. "Yes, about last night." He leaned over and adjusted the blotter on his desk.

He was nervous, Hank realized. Raymond always fussed when he was nervous. Hank wasn't sure if that made him feel any better, though. "I could apologize, if you would like. I could also offer my resignation if you would prefer."

Raymond froze. "What would you be apologizing for?" he asked cautiously, a politician to the very end. "Because," he went on in his most diplomatic voice, "if that was an attempt to smear my name and get something to hold over me, it won't work and I will accept your resignation, and then I will see Sheriff Cutler escort you out of town. Extortion is illegal here."

So that was it. Raymond was not just nervous, he was afraid. And with good reason. In Hank's time on Boston's mean streets, men who went for boys were always afraid of being found out. But their lust was greater than their fear and their money saved Hank from death.

"You have nothing to fear from me," he said, taking a step toward the desk—toward Raymond.

Raymond sucked in a little bit of air and held it. "So you say," he went on in a cool, dispassionate voice. "But what happened in this office last evening—that's a dangerous game to play. Careers and lives would be on the line."

Political doublespeak, all of it. "My loyalty lies

with you—you know that. It always has and I have yet to serve you wrong."

Color came to Raymond's cheeks, but otherwise, he showed no signs of comprehension. "You do good work for me. I feel that our business arrangement has been beneficial for both of us and I would hesitate before doing anything that would jeopardize that arrangement."

I don't want to mess this up. That's what Raymond meant. Hank appreciated the compliment, but he wanted a straight answer out of the man. "And you think that kissing me would 'jeopardize that arrangement,' as you say?"

The color spread to the tips of Raymond's ears and down the back of his neck, but finally, he looked directly at Hank. The intensity of his gaze—the longing that Hank saw there—it was a powerful, heady thing. "It could jeopardize everything."

Hank took another step closer. The space between them seemed to spark, like lightning striking out of a clear blue sky. "Aye, that it could. But I would not serve you wrong."

Raymond exhaled a shaky breath. "Are you a man of your word, Hank O'Shea? Because I would hold you to that."

Hank closed the rest of the distance between them and picked up Raymond's hand. He pressed it against his chest, right over his pounding heart. "Do you feel that?" he asked, watching the pulse in Raymond's neck flutter wildly. "That is what you do to me. And I can see that is what I do to you, too. I will not use you wrong. I swear that I will keep your secrets. No one will know, not by my lips."

Raymond's gaze dropped to his lips. That needed

no translation. But what he said next caught Hank off guard. "Miss Green sends her regards."

So the whore knew. "Do you trust her?" he asked, sliding his hand around the back of Raymond's neck. His skin was smooth under Hank's hands. Everything about Raymond was smooth. He was soft and unbroken by life and Hank would die before he let the world use this man as it had used him.

"Completely." Raymond's breath bounced off his cheek and Hank's knees weakened.

"Do you trust me?" The words were whispered against Raymond's lips, the promise of the kiss yet to come.

"Yes."

Yesterday, the kiss had been slow and hesitant, awkward and unsure. Today, however, was a different day.

Hank wouldn't have thought he could've forgotten what this was like—but then, it had never been like *this*. He'd had all kinds of sex, in nearly every way possible. This *was* different. Kissing Raymond was something else entirely—something he didn't recognize. It scared him, but he liked it. He liked the feel of Raymond's fingers burrowing into his unruly hair and tilting his head sideways for better access. And when Raymond opened his mouth for Hank, he knew this was more than mere *liking*. So much more.

He groaned into Raymond, struggling to keep control, but he was failing at that. He wrapped his arms around Raymond's waist, holding him tight to his chest, their bodies hot against each other. Raymond made a whimpering noise high in the back of his throat as their tongues tangled and Hank cupped his ass.

"Oh, God," Raymond moaned as Hank ground his erection against Raymond's. *Take* was the only thought that Hank could form. He wanted to take Raymond. He didn't want to wait anymore—he was so tired of waiting. "Is this really happening?"

Hank skimmed his hands around to where Raymond's cock was throbbing in his trousers. "Feels real to me," he said, palming Raymond's length.

Raymond gripped him by the shoulders. "I want this to be real. I don't want this to be a dream anymore."

How long had he been fantasizing about this moment? Longer than Hank had been, no doubt.

Hank backed him up until Raymond's ass hit the desk. Then he began to work at the buttons on Raymond's trouser front. "You hid it well."

"I had to."

"I know." He shoved the trousers aside and went to work on the drawstrings of Raymond's drawers. He dropped to his knees. He would do this first—show Raymond that he would not just take. He could give.

"Is… Is this what we do? Oh, God," he moaned as Hank freed his cock from his drawers and stroked up his length.

Hank looked up at him from the floor. Raymond looked impossibly innocent. "Haven't you ever had anyone suck you off before?" As he said it, he gave Raymond's tip a little squeeze and then, without breaking eye contact, leaned forward and kissed the tip.

Raymond's entire body convulsed. "No."

Hank stuck out his tongue and traced a small circle around Raymond's tip. "Not even Miss Green?"

Raymond shook his head, but when his mouth opened, no sound came.

It didn't seem possible that there was still innocence left this world and less possible that it existed in a place like Brimstone. For a second, Hank felt too dirty for this. Raymond was innocent and Hank was anything but. Hank had done things that would make the whores at the Jeweled Ladies faint with shock. Just because Hank tried to put his past aside didn't mean it didn't exist. If Raymond knew the truth about him, would he be repulsed? Would he kick Hank out of Brimstone rather than risk that, someday, someone might show up and know the truth?

Hank hesitated—but in that moment, Raymond reached down and stroked his fingertips over Hank's cheek. "If you show me what to do," he said, his voice shaky, "can I do it to you, too?"

No one stayed innocent forever and sinners had more fun. "Watch—but be quiet," Hank told him and then he finally, *finally*, took Raymond's cock into his mouth. The door was locked—but noise carried.

Raymond did as he was told—or, he tried to, anyway. Hank glanced up at him through his lashes and saw that he had his mouth firmly shut—but that didn't stop the moans. It was like watching the whole world wake up in his eyes, Hank thought as he bobbed his head up and down on Raymond's cock. Hank hadn't done this in so long—but it all came back to him. Better than before, too. Raymond's cock was hard and hot in his mouth—salty. Truthfully, Hank had been a little worried that he might not like this. He didn't have the fondest memories of sucking men off.

But Raymond wasn't just some paying man. He was *Raymond* and the taste of him danced on Hank's tongue.

32

This would be better if there were less clothes involved, but Hank worked with what he had. He gripped the base of Raymond's cock and, with his other hand, cupped his jewels through his pants. Raymond made noises that sounded like a teakettle getting ready to whistle, which made Hank smile.

When he'd first come to this country, this had been powerlessness. He'd been young and vulnerable and men had shoved their rods in him wherever they wanted and he'd taken it because he needed the money. It had only been when he'd turned sixteen and realized that he could use what he knew about those fine, upstanding members of Boston society to his advantage that he'd started to see his way out.

Extortion wasn't legal in Boston, either. It was, however, profitable.

But Raymond had closely guarded his secret for years—his entire life. He'd guarded it so well that Hank, who was used to all the signals that men sent out, hadn't even suspected for a long time and even when he had, he hadn't been sure of what he'd been seeing.

But this? This was a different kind of power. This wasn't just secrets and shame—this was something else. For the first time in his life, Hank felt like he was worth something. Raymond wanted him and, what's more, he thought Hank was worth the risk. Raymond hadn't had anyone else do this to him *ever*. It was something, being a man's first.

"Hank," Raymond ground out through gritted teeth. He fisted his hands in Hank's hair as if he couldn't decide if he wanted to push Hank away or pull him in closer. Seconds later, his hot spunk began

33

to spurt into Hank's mouth and Hank swallowed it greedily. He slowed his movements, still pulling on Raymond's cock, but more gently as he finished off in his mouth. And then, just like that, all the tension drained out of Raymond's body and he went limp. Hank barely caught him in his arms as he pivoted so that Raymond fell into the chair instead of onto the floor. Raymond slumped back in the chair, looking dazed and euphoric. With a shaky hand, he reached up and dragged his thumb over Hank's lips.

"Oh, God," he said in a voice little more than whisper. "We're going to go to hell for that, aren't we?"

"I don't mind, as long as you're there with me." He was just starting to realize that this didn't have to be a one-time thing. This could be something they shared for a long while, even.

Hank had spent years trying to make himself into something better. Suddenly, he could only pray that he was something good enough for Raymond Dupree.

The man in question was now grinning wildly. There weren't calculations behind the smile, nor regrets. Raymond was happy, pure and simple. And Hank had given that to him. It made him feel good in a way he hadn't expected.

"I don't know if I know how to do that," Raymond started hesitantly.

Hank heard the unspoken question. Raymond had admitted his innocence—and Hank had just demonstrated his complete lack thereof. "You don't have to try if you don't want." It was a painful offer to make, for his cock was rock hard and aching. He needed his release—and soon.

Raymond pulled him into a kiss. "I want to try but I know I won't be as good as you are."

The thought of Raymond's lips wrapping around his cock did things to him. "Are you sure?" That was his last attempt at chivalry. But even as he said it, he climbed to his feet and began working at his trouser buttons because he couldn't hold back, not for a second longer. If Raymond couldn't finish him, he'd finish himself.

"Tell me what to do," Raymond said, leaning forward and, after pausing for a second, slipping his hands underneath the drawstring of Hank's drawers. He was shaking as his hands closed around Hank's cock.

Hank's hips began to thrust on their own, sliding his cock through Raymond's loose grip. "Kiss it," he told Raymond as he leaned forward, bracing his hands on the back of Raymond's chair.

Raymond stared at his cock for a long time and Hank guessed that, outside of his own, it was the first time he had seen another man's cock up close. This innocence—this curiosity—it was killing him. Just when he couldn't take it another second, Raymond leaned forward and pressed his lips against the tip. Hank's cock twitched at the contact and he groaned.

Now was Raymond's turn to look up at him. "Shh," he scolded and then, God help Hank, he opened his mouth and took Hank's cock into his body.

It was so tempting just to thrust until he came fast and hard—but this wasn't the end of something. This was only the beginning. "Aye, like that," he agreed as quietly as he could. "Grip it harder." Raymond did as he was told. God, he was so beautiful sucking on Hank's cock. "Like you were stroking yourself."

Raymond's eyes drifted shut and he moaned around the head of Hank's cock. The noise shot through Hank's body like a drug. Only the beginning, he reminded himself. "Aye, you stroke yourself, don't you? Do you think of me when you do it, all alone in that big bed of yours?"

Raymond's movements were sloppy and awkward as he nodded—oh, but he made up for it with enthusiasm. "I think of you, too," Hank whispered. He would've thought that this wouldn't have affected him. Sex was just sex. There wasn't anything special about it. But this? Watching Raymond surround him with his wet mouth and look up at him as if Hank was making every single one of his dreams come true?

He must've thrust too hard because suddenly, Raymond choked and pulled away. "I'm sorry," he mumbled, still coughing.

Ah, hell. "It's okay, it's okay." He was frantic with need but he wouldn't force this, not like he'd been forced.

Raymond didn't push him away, didn't get a look of fear on his face. Hell, he didn't even let go of Hank's cock. Instead, he rested his head against the top of Hank's thigh. "I can do this, right?" he asked in an innocent voice as he gripped Hank with both hands and began to stroke up and down.

Ah, sweet Jesus. "Aye, you can. Just like you stroke yourself."

Raymond's grip on him tightened and Hank's ability to think dissolved into nothingness. This, at least, Raymond had a better handle on. Within moments, Hank was frantically trying to get his handkerchief out of his pocket before he exploded all over Raymond's suit. He barely made it in time before he let go.

When it was over and Hank waited for the feelings to hit. The dirtiness, the hollowness. For so long, men had treated him like this handkerchief—something to make a mess in and then toss away. Even the women, because there had been women, hadn't been much better.

But those feelings didn't come because Raymond looped his arms around Hank's waist and held him tight. A miracle, that. Such a simple touch.

Shaking, he pulled away and did up his pants. Raymond kept looking at him, a stunned look on his face. Hank felt much the same.

Hank moved without thinking. He grabbed Raymond and hauled him up, wrapping his arms around him and crushing him to his chest. "You beautiful man," he whispered as Raymond sank into his chest.

"I waited for you for so long."

And that made Hank happy, too. He was worth something—a lifetime of waiting. This was all new to him, but he liked it. "So you want to keep doing it, then?"

"I do." Raymond leaned back, joy all over him. But it went quicker than Hank would've liked. "God, I do. But we have to be careful. We have to keep this quiet."

"We have to have a plan," Hank agreed. And one was already forming in his mind.

Raymond said he trusted Emerald Green completely.

Hank needed to find out if that trust was misplaced or not.

Chapter Four

Emmy was in such a state that by Sunday morning, she could barely think. She had received her customary bouquet of flowers on Wednesday, but other than that she had not heard from Raymond. They didn't normally communicate outside of their evening—but circumstances had changed. She was dying to know what had happened between him and Hank and if her name had come up. She knew she had no claim to Raymond—she didn't want to lose him, though. But she did want him to be happy. It was all a mess inside of her head.

Which meant that, when a knock came on her door early Sunday morning, she almost fell out of her bed. "Yes?"

Mistress was standing before her. Even her day dress was a luminous pink silk and Emmy felt painfully underdressed in nothing but her wrapper. "You have a caller." But even as she said it, she seemed confused.

Emmy started. "At ten on a Sunday morning?" They did not normally receive gentlemen on Sundays. Mistress had long ago reasoned that her position within the community was more secure when she was not making a sacrilege of a holy day. And besides, business was always slow.

38

Emmy's first thought went to Raymond. "Is it Mayor Dupree?"

Mistress shook her head no. "The gentleman does not wish to join you in the bedroom," she said diplomatically. "He wishes to take tea with you in the parlor and nothing more. He was quite clear on that point."

Emmy's hand flew to her hair. She was not dressed for the parlor. She wasn't even dressed for the saloon. "Who is it, then?"

Mistress swallowed and it was then that panic took hold of Emmy. Was it the man who wanted to tie her—and only her—up and whip her?

Mistress smiled, but it was not a thing of happiness. It was her only outward sign of confusion. "Mr. Hank O'Shea. I believe he is Mayor Dupree's man of business?"

All Emmy could do for a few painful seconds was blink. Anything else would betray her surprise at this development. She had understood Raymond—she thought. Hank O'Shea had kissed Raymond. Why had he come for *her*? "Of course I will receive him," she said, her voice coming out slightly strangled sounding. "He will have to wait, however."

"Do you require assistance? I believe Ebony has not left for church, if you need help getting into your gown."

Emmy nodded and Mistress swirled away. Emmy hurried to her dressing table and began to pin up her hair. Why would Hank O'Shea be here? Had he come to warn her away from Raymond? She had heard rumors that Hank O'Shea could be brutish. Raymond had told her himself several times now he had needed

39

someone to feel the fear of God and Hank had been the man to do it. What if Mr. O'Shea *had* been the man who'd requested her time on Tuesday?

But his path and Emmy's had never crossed before. She didn't want to be afraid of him. She wanted to like him, for Raymond's sake.

An unannounced visit during her private hours, however, was not a good start.

Ebony slipped into her room. "A caller?" she asked quietly as she helped Emmy into the sprigged muslin gown Ebony had only finished a few weeks ago. The dress was pale green with pink flowers embroidered on the flounces. Emmy was tempted to put on her deep emerald green silk—but it was only ten on a Sunday.

"I'm not sure," Emmy admitted. She was Emerald Green, by God—she would not be comforted by Ebony's presence. She didn't need reassurances. She could handle a man like Hank O'Shea.

"We don't normally do anything on Sundays," Ebony said as she did up Emmy's buttons.

"I know. This is just... tea?" The two women looked at each other in the mirror, no doubt thinking the same thing.

Things that started with tea rarely ended there.

She was surprised when Ebony took her by the hands and laid a kiss on her cheek. "Be careful with him—and with the mayor. You're a dear friend and I..." Her eyes got misty.

"I will," Emmy promised as she pulled Ebony into a tight hug. She had always gotten on well with Ebony, but this concern was touching. "And no matter what, we will always be friends." That got Emmy a wonderful smile.

Besides, Emmy couldn't agree more. She wouldn't risk hurting Raymond, no matter what Mr. Hank O'Shea said or did. She would gladly face down dragons for Raymond.

Twenty minutes had passed before Emmy was ready—but Hank O'Shea could just wait. It was impolite for a gentleman to turn up unannounced on a lady. Even if Emmy wasn't a lady, it was still rude.

Finally, she could put it off no longer. She adjusted her bosom—really, this was one of her more prim gowns—and headed down to the parlor.

Hank O'Shea stood when she entered the room and for a moment, Emmy was taken aback. The man simply *filled* the parlor. It wasn't that he was the tallest man she had ever seen—but there was something about the way his jacket strained over his shoulders and his eyes smoldered at her that took all of the extra space in the room and tossed it to the side. She had seen brutes before, of course, and spread her legs for her fair share of them—she wasn't sure she'd ever seen a bruiser like this man with such intelligent eyes.

No wonder Raymond was drawn to him. Raymond was a gentleman, polished and refined. The man standing before her was *not* a man to be trifled with.

His eyes raked over her body, but Emmy did not allow herself to shiver. "Mr. O'Shea. What a surprise."

The very corner of his mouth moved into something that could've been a smile on a lesser man. "Miss Green. Your beauty far surpasses what I expected."

Emmy felt a pang of homesickness at the sound of the Irish in his voice. She hadn't heard the proper Irish accent since her mother had died and she missed it. But she shook off this unwanted sentimentality. "I pride myself on being something other than what people expect. Please, have a seat."

Mistress herself carried in the tea service—no doubt to keep a close eye on this irregular meeting. She made polite small talk with Hank while Emmy studied him out of the corner of her eye. Black Irish, she quickly concluded. His hair was midnight black and his eyes were a pale blue. There was a scar on his cheek and his knuckles looked like they had seen many a hard fight. A brawler, then. A man who, at one point, had fought for a living.

A dangerous man. And *this* was who Raymond had given his heart to? Could there be any gentleness in Hank O'Shea? Raymond would require some, at least part of the time.

Emmy waited until Mistress had left them alone. "To what do I owe the pleasure of your visit today, Mr. O'Shea?"

The corner of his mouth moved again. "I thought it was time for our paths to cross."

That told her nothing about why he was here. She took a sip of tea and set her cup back on the saucer, letting the moment stretch. "And now they have." She waited. She owed this man nothing.

"You have spirit." It was a meaningless compliment, so she didn't deign to reply. "I suppose you've guessed why I'm here," he finally added.

"I assure you, Mr. O'Shea, I haven't the first notion."

He gave her a full smile—and Emmy knew immediately that it was not a true smile. Instead, it was the kind of look a wolf might give a deer. It was a shame that Mr. O'Shea had not yet realized she was not prey. "I'll give you a thousand dollars if you turn Raymond away next Tuesday."

This statement so confounded her that all she could do was stare at him, her mouth open in unladylike horror. "I beg your pardon?"

Hank shrugged in a casual manner that did not match the look in his eyes. "You're a bit of a liability, Miss Green. Raymond has grand plans for his political career and it is my job to make sure that he sees his plans to the end. You've been good for him—no one would argue that. But he needs to move on if he wants to get out of Brimstone."

Because she was in the parlor, Emmy did not throw her cup of hot tea in his face nor did she dump the teapot into his lap, although he richly deserved it. Instead, she gracefully stood to her feet and forced a placid smile to her face. "Thank you for stopping by, Mr. O'Shea. While your offer is most generous, I believe I shall pass."

He moved before she could react. His hand clamped around her wrist—and he hadn't even stood to do it. His arms were just that long. Her skin heated at his touch—an unusual enough reaction—but she chalked it up to fear. "I thought you were a whore."

She did not wrench her hand away from his grip. She did nothing that would betray her emotions. Instead, as haughtily as she could, she looked down at where he held her fast and waited for him to remove his hand. To his credit, he did so after only a few seconds. "I shall thank you not to use such language in the parlor." Her voice shook with anger, dammit.

43

"Think of what you could do with a thousand dollars, Emmeline."

Her cheeks heated even as a chill raced down her back. How did he know her name? Even Raymond called her Emmy. No one in this town—in this state—knew who she really was, aside from Mistress.

Or so she thought. Apparently, she had thought wrong.

"You could stop being Emerald Green," he went on in a low voice as he stood. "You could go back to being Emmeline McCartney. You could buy yourself a nice house or piece of land. You wouldn't have to spread your legs anymore. You could be a free woman with that kind of money."

She was physically shaking with rage because of course she wanted that. But to turn away Raymond? The one man she could count as a friend?

She knew what this was. Jealousy. "And you call yourself his friend?"

If he were insulted by this, he didn't show it. He lifted an eyebrow at her. "I call him many things. He needs a wife if he's going to be governor and you, my dear lady, are not that woman."

She had the distinctive feeling that she was being baited. Well, Hank O'Shea had no idea who he was up against. Emerald Green could not be baited. She affixed her frostiest smile to her face. "And you are?"

Something in his eyes shifted—an appreciation? It was a shame she didn't like him because, in all honesty, he was an intensely handsome man. If one liked brutes, that was.

"I must respectfully decline your generous offer," she said in a severe voice. There was no respect involved in this and they both knew it. "If Mr. Dupree chooses to end our friendship, I trust that he is man enough to tell me himself instead of relying on his lapdog."

O'Shea took a step toward her and prickles of awareness skittered down her back. But she did not cower before him. She cowered before no man.

He took her chin in between his thumb and forefinger and tilted her head from side to side. "You really are beautiful, Emmeline. The bonniest lass I've seen in an age. And you're yet young. You may think you love him, but you know he can't give you what you really need. You could start a new life far away from here, find a good man who could satisfy you in bed." His gaze dropped to her lips. "And out of it."

Emmy was proud of the way that she did not stiffen at his touch. "Many a man has offered to take me away from all this, Mr. O'Shea. This may come as a shock to you, but I enjoy my position here at the Jeweled Ladies and in Brimstone. I enjoy my relationship with Raymond. I do not, however, enjoy your company. So you will excuse me if I fail to bid you a good day." She gave a little curtsy, which had the additional benefit of pulling her face away from his hand and then turned to go.

"My offer stands," he said behind her. "One thousand by end of business Wednesday."

She should just walk away, for he was clearly not worth her time. But, somehow, Raymond loved this beast. So, for Raymond, she turned back and said in a quiet voice, "Why are you doing this?"

"He needs to marry the right woman. Cynthia Hobbs, maybe."

"She will never understand him," Emmy said severely. Surely, if Hank had kissed Raymond, he understood that. "If you cared for him, you would not ask this of me."

He came up to her then, his body close enough that the heat from his chest radiated. This man could have anyone he wanted. Did he truly want Raymond? "It's because I care for him that I'm asking." He lifted his hand and brushed his thumb over her cheek. His touch invoked the oddest reaction in her—a strange fluttering that started where his skin touched hers and rippled like waves in a pond throughout her body. "And I care for you. You should have more happiness than a man who can wed you, but can't bed you."

Men lied to her all the time and she, in return, did the same. Their wives didn't understand them and she loved sleeping with them. Her gentlemen callers paid her to make those lies believable; they paid her well. But a thousand dollars?

No. She wasn't engaging in that transaction, not with this man. "You care nothing for me, Mr. O'Shea. Do not pretend otherwise." She turned to leave again and this time, he did not stop her.

"Think about it," he called as she swept from the room.

She did not reply.

*

This week, Raymond was early for his appointment with Emmy. He all but floated into the Jeweled Ladies because he'd spent the last week with Hank in his arms.

46

Oh, not literally. They went about their day much the same as they always did. But it was at the end of the day when things changed. When Hank was positive that no one would come looking for them, they locked themselves in Raymond's office and quickly dispensed with the pleasantries. A day's worth of frustrations needed to be relieved and relieved *immediately*.

It still amazed him how much of a difference there was between him stroking himself and Hank stroking him. In theory, it was the same action. A tight grip, an up-and-down motion until completion. But in application, the difference was stunning. Hank knew how to do things with his mouth that Raymond had never dreamed of. Raymond had no hope of being as good with his tongue as Hank was—but Hank did not seem to mind.

Instead, he crushed Raymond in his arms and told him how beautiful, how perfect he was. And today? Today he had whispered that he loved Raymond.

Love. Something Raymond had never thought possible, and now here it was. A careful, quiet love, but love nonetheless.

He couldn't wait to tell Emmy about it. Finally, he knew what she knew—the acts of physical intimacy were something rare and special. Oh, all right— perhaps her particular brand of physical intimacy was less than rare and occasionally not special. But it was all so new to him and he needed to tell *someone*.

But in the parlor, she was quiet. It was only when they had stripped down to their underclothes and were in tucked into bed together that she said, "I have to tell you something."

"What?" The concern in her voice snapped him

47

out of his reverie. Was she leaving? Or—more disastrously—was she with child?

"Are you sure you can trust Hank?" Her voice was so quiet that he had to lean even closer than he already was to hear her.

"After this week? There is no question about that." Still, she sounded worried. And that worried him. "Why?"

She exhaled heavily and he felt a tremor pass through her body. "He came to see me on Sunday."

"He did?" Hank had not mentioned that to him.

"Yes. And he offered me a thousand dollars to turn you away tonight. He said I could take the money, go somewhere and start over. I wouldn't have to be a whore anymore—so long as I turned you away." She looked up at him and he saw tears in her eyes.

"He said *what*?"

She nodded, looking like a widow grieving. "He told me that you would need a wife because you were going to be governor one day and I couldn't be that for you. And I know that I can't—I *know* that." A sob tried to break free from her, but she smothered it. "But I know you can't be happy with Cynthia Hobbs, either."

His stomach turned. "What—why? Why would he do that?"

"He knew things, Raymond." The blood drained from her face. "He knew my name. He said I wouldn't have to be Emerald Green anymore."

Of course Raymond knew that Emerald Green wasn't Emmy's name. But the fact that Hank knew something about this woman that Raymond didn't— that rankled. "Did he threaten you?" Because that was unacceptable.

"No. At least... not directly. He just..."

"Tell me, darling."

"He made it sound like he wanted me to be happy. I could find a man and get married. Someone who could take care of me."

Raymond swallowed. "I can take care of you." In all ways. Except for one.

She propped herself up on his chest and stared down at him. "I love you, Raymond. You know that, don't you?"

He smiled, but sadness gripped him. He brushed her red curls away from her face. "And I, you, Emmy. I would marry you tomorrow, if I could."

A tear spilled over and ran a path down her face. "I need a man in my bed, Raymond. Not just what we have here. You understand now, don't you? You and Hank..."

They had done things—things with mouths and hands and rods. And if Raymond had to suddenly not do those things ever again...

He didn't know if he could go back to the way things had been before. He wasn't the same person, not anymore.

"You could take lovers. We both could."

She shook her head. "No, because people would find out. Someone would talk and then the gossip would spread like a grassfire and your career would crumble to ashes, Raymond. What kind of leader lets his wife—a former whore—cuckold him?" She shook her head again. "I can't do that to you. I can't drag you down. And if I got pregnant—then what? You'd raise a bastard baby as your own?"

"I'm not going to father a child. The thought of doing that with someone—"

49

"Cynthia Hobbs," she interrupted quietly. "That's who Hank would choose for you."

Bile rose up in the back of his throat. He'd thought he understood Hank—but this? Trying to buy Emmy off? Insisting that Raymond should marry Cynthia? It went too far. "Your child would be mine, no matter what. Even now—if you were carrying right now, Emmy, I'd claim you and the babe as my own."

"But, Raymond—your career..." She sat up on her knees and cupped his face in her hands. "I wish I could be everything you need me to be. I would do anything to be that wife for you."

He sat up and said, "And I wish I could be the man you need, Emmy."

She leaned in. "Could we try? Just this once..."

Raymond nodded. "Just this once." And only because it was Emmy. Because he did love her, in a fashion. If only he could...

Emmy slid into his lap, straddling him. Her hair tumbled from its loosened pins over her shoulders. Her shift had slipped and her left shoulder was bare. She was simply the most beautiful woman he'd ever seen—but lust was slow to come, if it came at all.

She cupped his face in her hands and pulled him in closer. Her lips touched his and he willed his rod to react. It wasn't unpleasant, her kiss. It was much the same as lying in bed with her. Soft, sweet—but his rod refused to move. Not a jump, not a twitch.

Instead, his traitorous mind went right back to the traitorous Hank. Raymond didn't know what game Hank was playing, but he was going to put a stop to it. As Emmy kissed him, he prayed long and hard that she had just misunderstood Hank, that was all.

But Emmy was not a stupid woman and Hank...

Raymond didn't know enough about Hank. Hell, he hadn't even known Emmy's name.

So he tried harder. He wrapped his arms around her waist and sucked at her lower lip the way Hank sucked at his. He hesitated and then cupped her breast in his hands, letting its heavy weight fill his palm. She shifted her hips, her heat brushing against his limp rod. And...

"Anything?" she asked after several minutes.

"Nothing," Raymond shook his head sadly as he sank back into the pillows. "It was not bad," he told her, trying to soften the blow. "The thought of doing that with any other woman is terrible and with you, I don't mind." He waved his hand over his lifeless rod. "But as you can see..."

"Nothing," she said in disappointment.

They lay back down and Emmy pulled the covers over them both. "It was pleasant," she told him. "But there wasn't a spark."

"So we are agreed?"

"I would say so." No marriage because there could be no passion. "What shall we do now?"

"We will continue on."

"What about Hank?" She wrapped her arms around his waist and hugged him tight. "I do not want him to use you ill, Raymond. You deserve better than that."

"I'll deal with him. He will not threaten you."

They lay in silence for a long time, two bodies sharing the warmth of friendship—and little more. And something itched at Raymond's mind.

"Emmy?"

"Yes?"

"What is your name?"

"Emmeline," she sighed. "Emmeline McCartney was who I used to be. My mother called me Emmy. You are the only person I allow to use that name."

So she had been sharing a part of her when she'd told him to call her that. Raymond felt a bit better.

"Be careful with Hank," she said quietly. "There is something about him—he said he was offering me money because he cared for you. But I cannot see how making a true friend leave you is caring."

That was it, wasn't it? Because Raymond couldn't see it, either. But he was going to find out, one way or the other.

Hank had sworn he would not use Raymond ill.

Raymond was going to hold him to that.

Chapter Five

Raymond wasn't sure he'd ever been so mad. His world was colored red at the edges and it was all because of Hank.

Hank, his trusted second. Hank, the man he loved.

Hank, the man who'd threatened Emmy.

Raymond didn't know if he wanted to strangle the man or call him out or… or what. But he was going to get to the bottom of this. Starting right now.

Which was why he was storming toward Mabel Bund's boarding house only a little past nine on Tuesday night. Normally, he stayed with Emmy until midnight. But after the failed attempt at a kiss, he hadn't been able to contain himself. Hank had to answer for this. Immediately.

Yes, Hank had occasionally intimidated people or taken care of a 'problem' for Raymond. But this? Trying to buy Emmy off? Deciding who Raymond would marry?

Marry? Hell! He didn't want to marry anyone. If he had to, he'd marry Emmy because he could at least kiss her at the front of a church without gagging. He knew he couldn't do that with Cynthia Hobbs or any of the other marriageable young ladies in this town.

Dammit, he'd just discovered Hank as a lover. For

the first time, Raymond had been comfortable with who he was and what he wanted, all because Hank was like… well, the man was permission. It was still a sin, what he and Hank did together. But it felt less damning because Raymond wasn't the only one coveting.

Why on God's green earth would the man do something like this—to Emmy, of all people? The one person Raymond could trust? Couldn't Raymond get more than seven days of happiness? Or was this the price to pay for his sin?

Hank was his assistant and his lover, but he did not run Raymond's life. Not like this. And if that was going to be a problem, Hank would find himself outside city limits by dawn.

But Raymond didn't want that, either, because if he had to remove Hank, when would he get another chance at a lover? He wouldn't. He'd have to marry someone and spend the rest of his life pretending to be something he wasn't. It wouldn't be awful if that someone was Emmy, but she was right. If they each took a lover and someone talked, they'd both be ruined.

He banged on Mrs. Bund's door, trying to calm himself. God, how he wanted Hank. But he couldn't lose Emmy. The woman had saved his sanity and, quite possibly, his life.

"Yes?" Mrs. Bund's face appeared at a crack in the door. "Oh! Mayor Dupree!" Her wrinkled face creased with worry. "Is everything all right?" Her thick German accent burred the words together.

"Fine," he assured her with a forced smile. He could only hope he didn't look like a raving madman. "But I need to speak with Mr. O'Shea. Is he in?" As the words left his mouth, Raymond considered the possibility that Hank would be out. This was Raymond's night to be with Emmy. Maybe Hank had other plans? Or even other lovers?

Raymond's stomach turned. He'd given himself to Hank O'Shea, but there was so much he didn't know. Had he made a mistake?

He didn't know who he was mad at—Hank, or himself. Because if he hadn't trusted Hank, neither Raymond nor Emmy would be in this situation.

"He's in. I'll fetch him for you," Mrs. Bund said.

As he waited, Raymond grappled with the uncomfortable truth that he could have single-handedly ruined his life. A week of satisfaction—and it could be the end of his career.

Just then, Hank appeared in the doorway and the red rage that Raymond had diligently been pushing against came flooding back.

The next thing he knew, he had Hank by the shirt. "What did you do?" he snarled—actually snarled—in Hank's face.

He didn't know what he expected Hank to do— but ask, "Did she turn you away?" with a look of concern on his face wasn't it.

Raymond shook him. Hank wasn't exactly a rag doll, but he put up no resistance. "You offered her—"

Did Hank look... relieved? "*Shh.*"

Confusion momentarily halted Raymond's assault. "What?"

"I'll come with you." But before Raymond could tell him *no*, he'd pitched his voice up. "Let me get my hat. I'm sure we'll get this settled by morning."

"What the hell are you talking about?" he hissed.

"Not here." And with that, he slipped back into the house, leaving Raymond off balance.

"Is everything all right, Mayor Dupree? It's not Indians, is it?" Mrs. Bund lived in fear of an Indian attack.

"No, no—nothing serious," he said trying to sound reassuring. "But Mr. O'Shea's assistance is required."

Mrs. Bund glanced over her shoulder. "I should be careful, Mayor. Mr. O'Shea is Irish, you know."

Despite the situation, Raymond almost laughed. That was the least dangerous thing about the man. "Yes, I was aware."

Hank appeared, settling his bowler hat firmly over his black hair. He had his leather case in his hand and he looked like he was on his way to an emergency meeting. "Don't wait up, Mrs. Bund," he said, smoothly stepping around her. "Ready?"

Ready for what? Because honestly, Raymond had expected something different out of Hank. He'd expected belligerence or denial—not this concern and relief.

"Are your servants at home?" Hank asked in a quiet voice as they strode away from the boarding house.

"No. It's Tuesday." Neither the cook nor the maid lived in his house, but his night with Emmy meant Mary and Mrs. Newsome had the afternoon off. Neither would be back until Mrs. Newsome came in to cook breakfast at six tomorrow morning. Mary would most likely arrive at eight—if that. "But if you think you're staying, you've got another think coming."

Hank snorted. "You're upset."

Raymond stopped in the middle of the street, so 'upset' he almost couldn't speak. "You're damned right I'm—"

But Hank interrupted him with a look. "Wait until we get to your place. Yell at me then," he said, before motioning for Raymond to continue.

Raymond glowered at him. "I will. Don't think I won't." He choked his rage down and focused on keeping a mild expression on his face.

Hank was right, of course. To have this out in public was a poor idea. But it galled Raymond that the man could be strolling along next to him as if they were rushing to a late-night meeting.

It was only when Raymond had let Hank into his house and shot the bolt behind them that he exploded again. "How could you do that?" he demanded.

Hank looked contrite. Where was the brawler who refused to take guff from anyone? "She didn't turn you away, though?"

"Of course she didn't," Raymond spat out. There was a part of him that wanted Hank to fight back. He wanted Hank to defend himself so that Raymond could be properly mad all over again. "But offering her money to turn me aside? What—*why*?" he sputtered. "Why, goddamnit?"

"Because I needed to be sure I could trust her." If Hank had thought this admission would help his cause, he was sorely mistaken.

Raymond grabbed him by the jacket lapels and had shoved him back against the door. "I told you I trusted her and she proved true."

"She told you everything? How much I offered her?"

"Of course she did," he ground out, shaking Hank. "A thousand dollars because I have to marry someone like Cynthia Hobbs. Because Emmy's a whore who'll destroy my career." Raymond was not a violent man and he rarely got angry—and certainly not angry enough to strike a man. But right now, he was thinking about punching Hank right in the mouth. "That's what you told her, isn't it?"

"Good."

"Good?" Confusion warred with anger, leaving Raymond hot under the collar. He had Hank pressed back against his front door and suddenly, he was aware they were completely alone in the privacy of his own home.

Hank nodded, his gaze dropping to Raymond's lips. "We can trust her."

No, he wasn't going to let Hank's mouth distract him. Raymond jerked him forward and slammed him back against the door, trying to focus on his anger. It didn't work, not entirely. Because a new emotion bubbled up between the anger and the confusion—lust. Raymond went hard. In the last week, Raymond had been eager, but timid. This, though—this was passion. Raw, pure passion and it excited him.

"You trust her? Tell me this, Hank—why should *we* trust *you*?"

"Think about what I did," Hank reasoned, sounding damnably calm. But even as he spoke, he rested his hands on Raymond's waist. "If she'd taken the money, you would have been well rid of her. She could have been bought off—someone else could have paid her for what she knows about us."

"*What?*"

"If she refused my offer—then we both know how loyal she is," he went on. "She has sex for money—and I offered her an obscene amount of money. But she loves you, don't you see? She loves you more than that."

Some of Raymond's anger blurred away. "She does. She told me so."

"So now we know. She can keep our secrets, yours and mine." As he said it, he pulled Raymond's waist against his. Raymond could feel Hank's rod as hard as his own.

He refused to give into the lust because this was more important. He slammed Hank into the door again, harder this time. But the man just took it, an odd look on his face. "Fight back," Raymond growled because he knew damned good and well that Hank let no man intimidate him.

"No," Hank said simply. His hands tightened on Raymond's waist, but he didn't push him away. Instead, he pulled Raymond in closer. Their erections rubbed against each other again.

"Damn your hide, *fight back*." Hank just shook his head. "Why the hell not?" Raymond's breath was coming harder now and fury had nothing to do with it.

"I won't hurt you, Raymond." He whispered it with such tenderness that Raymond almost cried right then and there.

"But you did." He couldn't make sense of this. His body was warring with his mind—and his heart was apparently going to be the first casualty. "You *did*—you tried to push Emmy away from me."

"I'm trying to protect you," he whispered. His hands moved and he cupped Raymond's face. "I

59

wanted to make sure she was worthy of you. You don't know how special you are, Raymond." Hank pulled him in closer, his breath warm on Raymond's lips. "God, I'd do anything for you."

"Why should I trust you?" Because that was what it all came back to—his heart, his head and his rod— Hank was asking for all of Raymond.

And Raymond wanted to give it all to Hank. Heart and soul, he was already Hank's, come hell or high water.

Hank pushed him back—but not away. Instead, in the little space he opened between their bodies, Hank fell to his knees, his fast hands undoing the buttons on Raymond's trousers and the drawstring on his drawers in mere seconds. "I'll take care of you. I promise, Raymond—let me take care of you." He shoved Raymond's clothes down, baring his ass and his legs. But he didn't take Raymond's rod in hand. Instead, he sat back on his heels and stared up at Raymond. *"Please."*

It was as if a spirit possessed Raymond. He sank his fingers into Hank's dark hair and jerked his head toward Raymond's rod. It was part lust, part punishment.

Hank complied. He took Raymond in his mouth and began to suck with an intensity that Raymond had only caught glimpses of in their week of illicit lovemaking. He wasn't holding back—and Raymond didn't have to, either.

"Oh, God," he moaned, both a prayer and a benediction, because he was surely going to hell for this and he was going to enjoy burning. But then, he'd been damned from the moment when, at the age of ten, he'd realized he was far more in love with the boy next door than his older, well-developed sister.

This was what he hadn't known he'd wanted then—but as he pumped his hips and thrust into Hank's hot, wet mouth, he knew now. This was what he'd been looking for out of the corner of his eye for his entire life—unbridled passion. Permission to want what he wanted. Permission to get it.

His whole life, he'd been looking for Hank O'Shea.

Hank looked up at him through his thick eyelashes as Raymond's rod moved in and out of his mouth. And he—he smiled. The man *smiled* around Raymond's rod as Raymond thrust faster and faster. He was happy to take this punishment, Raymond realized—because it wasn't a punishment at all. Hank wanted this at least as much as Raymond did. More, maybe.

Hank's hands moved. He squeezed Raymond's jewels, causing Raymond to shudder. Then one hand moved back farther, stroking the sensitive skin of Raymond's hole. It shouldn't have felt good—but Hank's gentle touch caused Raymond's muscles to clench which, in turn, pushed the pleasure higher and higher.

Raymond had to lean forward against the door as Hank moaned around his rod. It was too much—the sucking, the touching, the moaning. Everything happened all at once and suddenly he was spurting into Hank's mouth.

Hank sucked slower as Raymond finished—and then he was moving. His hands left Raymond's body and it took several seconds for Raymond to realize that

Hank had pulled his rod free of his clothes and was jerking on it in short, hurried pulls. Before Raymond could even make sense of this, Hank's eyes had rolled back in his head and he was spending his seed.

Raymond watched, fascinated. Would he ever get tired of this? Of watching Hank's thick rod quiver?

"Why did you do that?" he asked, his voice shaky. Because for the last week, Raymond had done it for him. He wasn't as good as Hank was, but he could still make Hank spend. It was a point of personal pride, how far he'd come in just a few short days.

"Because I want you too much," Hank said and, for the first time, he sounded unsure of himself. He slid out from underneath Raymond and climbed to his feet. There, he wavered, ever so slightly. "I'm not good enough for you, Raymond. You're good and pure and—"

"Less than pure now," he murmured, hauling his trousers up.

Hank wrapped his arms around Raymond's chest and pulled him in tight. "Listen to me, damn it, man. I know what I am. I could hurt you, don't you understand? I want…" his voice trailed off. "There are things you don't know."

Raymond tensed. "About you?"

"About me, about this—sex between two men."

That made him snort. "As if I know a great deal about sex between a man and a woman."

That made Hank smile. "Too pure, you are." He rested his head against Raymond's shoulder, but as much as Raymond wanted to sink into his arms, he held himself back. Hank sighed. "Let's have it out, then."

Chapter Six

Y ou knew her name."

Hank didn't particularly want to have this conversation in Raymond's entry hallway. Although the hall was nicer than Hank's room back at Mrs. Bund's boarding house. The wallpaper was a complicated floral pattern and the rug on the floor had been thick under his knees. Even in nothing but the moonlight streaming in through a side window, the woodwork gleamed with polish. Raymond's family home didn't scream quality— but it didn't have to.

"I had to be sure." He motioned down the hallway. "Maybe we could have some coffee?" He'd prefer to go straight upstairs—but he knew Raymond and he knew that the man would need something to do with his hands while he decided Hank's fate.

Raymond stiffened. "Fine." He pulled away from Hank and took off down the hall.

It pleased Hank to see that Raymond could make his own coffee. The man had no need to—he'd grown up in this fine house with servants and a family who could take care of his every need. He had money and power—things Hank hadn't had.

As he worked, Raymond said, "Complete honesty, Hank. If you can't give that to me, then we don't have anything."

Hank pulled up a chair and sat at a kitchen table. Even here, back in what was considered the servants' area, the table was polished and beautiful—not a burn mark or knife scar in sight. For God's sake, the chair didn't even squeak as he settled his frame into it. "Aye. So ask."

"What's your name? Your real name?"

"Moynihan," he said with a sigh. The name was old, part of a different life that had ended a long time ago. "My name was Henry Moynihan."

"Why do you go by Hank O'Shea?"

Complete honesty was going to be harder than he'd anticipated. Of course Hank had realized that Raymond would want the truth. But in his mind, actually forming the words hadn't been this hard. "Because Henry Moynihan is dead. Or he should have been." A hundred times over, he should have died on the streets. Starved to death, or frozen in the cruel Boston winter—or beaten senseless. He'd come close a few times, but he'd survived. He always would.

"What does that mean?" Raymond turned to glare at him. "Out with it. I'm not going to play this guessing game with you, Hank."

Hank gave him a long look, but bless the man, he didn't buckle. Most everyone else—men and women— would have. But Raymond, for his easy life and kind heart, was stronger than that. "I stowed away on a ship bound for Boston when I was twelve."

"Why?"

Hank couldn't keep the bitter smile off his face— or the bitterness out of his voice. "I was nothing but another mouth to feed. My ma had another babe—nine after me—and I was too big for the mines. No one would give me work and my da wasn't a kind man." Raymond gasped, but Hank went on. If they were going to have this out, then it all had to be out.

"I ran away. I'd heard all the stories about America. Streets paved with gold, milk and honey—it sounded a far sight better than starving in the famine. Only..." He scratched at the back of his neck. "Only Boston wasn't any better. And I was still starving."

"Did you know? I mean," Raymond said, rising to get the coffee cups, "did you know you liked men or... or was that choice made for you? I've known since I was maybe ten, at least."

Hank mulled that over. He'd had a friend back home in Dublin, Toby. He'd never kissed Toby, but he'd asked the boy to run away with him because it'd been almost too much to bear to leave him. But Toby had a good family and hadn't wanted the adventure of running away with Henry because he hadn't loved Henry the same way.

No, there wasn't a single thing of Hank's life in Ireland he missed—except for Toby. "I liked boys. But I hadn't acted on it until Boston."

"No?" He set the mugs down and immediately began fiddling with them.

"I like women just as much as I like men." His thoughts turned to Emerald Green—Emmeline. Her porcelain skin, her bright red hair—looking at her had been like looking at home. She'd been indignant but refined—and every bit as beautiful as she was rumored to be. And that was while she was dressed in a demure dress, fit for church. How would she look, tousled and flushed from sex? "Maybe even more."

Raymond's cheeks shot bright red. "I didn't—I mean—oh, hell."

Hank laughed at that. "I tell you this, my beautiful man, I like you. I'd thought that I wouldn't fall for a man, but I fell for you. I didn't want to, but here we are."

Raymond ducked his head, clearly pleased. But then he schooled his features into a scowl. "Don't change the subject at hand. What else do I need to know about you?"

Hank rose to check on the coffee. "Boston was rough, on the streets. I nearly died many times over."

Raymond looked horrified. "How did you survive?"

The coffee was ready. He turned back to the table. "The same way Emmy survives."

"You mean—you..." His cheeks, his ears—everything was red on the man.

Hank swallowed nervously. Because Raymond was too impossibly pure—and Hank was a sinner of the first order.

"Aye, I sucked men off for money. A man approached me on the street and offered me two dollars to..." his voice trailed off and they sat in silence for a moment. "I took the money," he added with finality. "And it wasn't all bad. Some of those men were good to me. And it was mostly men, in those first few years."

Of course, not all of them were. Some wanted more than a handsome boy—they wanted fear or pain. But Hank had learned to breathe through the worst of it and take comfort in the good times. He could disassociate from what was happening if he had to, but he sure as hell didn't want to do that with Raymond. Not ever with Raymond.

66

"But then I grew and women began to take notice—and I began to notice them." He sat down again, willing himself not to look at Raymond. "I know it doesn't make you happy to hear this, Raymond. But it is my truth. Although it's been a shite life, I'm still rather fond of it. Brought me to you, it did."

They sat in silence for a long time. Hank focused on his coffee and tried not to think more than the next five minutes ahead. Raymond could tell him it didn't matter, the things he'd done. Or he could draw down on him, kick him out of town. Or... or something in between, he didn't know what.

"How did you get out? That's... that's a hard life to get past."

Hank snorted. "I got smarter. I thought men paid for me to suck them off. But what they were really paying for was my silence. Silence, it turns out, is worth more than some spunk." He glanced at Raymond. If the man was going to throw hot coffee in his face, he wanted to dodge.

Raymond paled. "You *blackmailed* them?"

Hank shrugged, trying to keep calm first. "Don't think of it as blackmail. Think of it as... a price adjustment. My services got more valuable. *I* got more valuable. All those men... they were men of quality. They had what I wanted—respect and power, safety and security. But I had power, too. I knew who they were. I could name them."

Unsurprisingly, Raymond looked horrified. "Is that what's happening here?"

Hank sighed. "Raymond, I can't say it any plainer." He leaned over and covered Raymond's fidgeting hand with his, stilling it. "I've fallen for you."

67

"How can I be sure?" he whispered, but he didn't pull his hand away.

"You can't. You have to take me at my word."

Raymond looked at him askance. "You tell me you blackmailed men in Boston—and then ask me to trust you?"

Hank grinned. "But that wasn't me. That was Henry Moynihan. Hank O'Shea was born when I was twenty-two. I had saved up my ill-gotten money and headed west. I wound up here. I want to be a man of quality, someone people respect instead of fear."

Raymond pulled his hand away. "I don't want to be your means to an end, Hank."

"You aren't."

Raymond dropped his head into his hands. "This is too much, Hank. You were—you were *used* on the streets of Boston and blackmailing men—"

"And women." Which did not help.

Raymond glared at him. "And women. Women like Emmy?"

Hank shook his head. "Of course not. Call it... a professional courtesy."

"Oh, God." He looked miserable and it killed Hank that he had to break this news to Raymond. But better from him than from someone else. "And here?"

"What about here?"

"Who else do you see?"

"*Raymond.*" He looked up at Hank, his eyes shining bright. "You. I only see you. I've only seen *you* for the last two years. And no one for the year before that."

He could see Raymond struggling. And it was a great deal to take in.

Hank wasn't good with words but dammit, he had to try. "I look at you and… and I see the man I want to be. You're good and kind and fair and I'm none of those things. But I want to be better than I am. When I started, it was to rise above my station. But now?" He reached out his hand toward Raymond. "I do the things you can't because you're too good to get your hands dirty. But I'm not. That's why I'm here. I can be your instrument." He swallowed. "If you let me, I can be your everything."

Hank didn't know how long they sat there, his hand outstretched to Raymond and Raymond staring at it. "If I don't?"

Hank turned his hand over, but he didn't pull it away. "Then I'll leave. California. I'll start over again. I'll survive."

Raymond squeezed his eyes shut and the silence stretched. "And…" he said in a voice so quiet Hank had to lean forward to catch his words. "And if I do? If I ask you to stay?"

This—this was the part that made Hank unsure of himself. "You aren't going to like this."

Raymond pulled back. "What?"

"You need to marry Emmy."

"What?" He stood so fast his chair flipped backward.

"Marry her, Raymond. You'll never find a better woman."

"I—she—we *can't*." He sounded so despairing of this that Hank thought he might cry. "She needs a lover and I can't. I just *can't*. She won't cuckold me because the truth could slip out." He straightened. "She won't do that to me and I can't ask her to be celibate the rest of her life."

69

Hank thought back to the icy woman who'd cut him several times over in the short course of a ten-minute visit—if that. Beautiful, refined—but a whore. If Hank showed interest in her, she'd still be a whore.

But if Raymond married her... he'd lift her up. He'd make her the lady she was born to be. In public, Emmeline Dupree would be the highest of quality women.

In private...

"She wouldn't have to be celibate," he told Raymond, forcing his thoughts away from what Emmy looked like undressed.

Raymond glared at him. "I cannot satisfy her. Trust me on this. I *tried*."

He could just imagine. Poor Raymond, trying to feel something—*anything*—for Emmy. They made a pretty picture—but he had a better one. Hank stood. "If I can figure out a solution—one that keeps all of us happy—then will you consider marrying her?"

Raymond looked up at him, trust warring with suspicion. "I couldn't marry anyone else. You know that."

He looked at his pocket watch. Ten thirty in the evening. He could stay for a while longer without having to come up with a cover story for Mrs. Bund. "One thing at a time, Raymond." He held out his hand, intent on taking this man upstairs and stripping him down.

For the longest moment, Raymond looked at his hand and Hank began to despair. But then he stood and took Hank's hand in his.

"I trust you, Hank." His grip tightened. "But she has to agree. I won't coerce her."

Hank's mind began to spin. Raymond's salty spunk running down his throat—and Emmy's red hair unbound.

"I'll make it work," he promised. "You'll see."

Chapter Seven

A*ll is well."*
 That was the entirety of the note she
received with a bouquet of flowers Wednesday
morning. The note was in Raymond's hand, so there
was that.

But...

All was well?

What on earth did that mean? Had he spoken with
Hank? Had he—what? Defended Emmy's honor?
Dueled with Hank? Or...

Had Hank somehow managed to convince
Raymond that it had all been a misunderstanding?

Emmy did not think so. She had not
misunderstood that brute one bit. He'd tried to pay her
to disappear and she hadn't. She had spent more than a
few hours since trying to guess what Hank O'Shea
would do next. Would he confront her? Offer her more
money?

Or... there were whispers, after all, spoken behind
fans and by men deep in their cups about how Hank
made problems 'disappear' for Raymond.

This thought panicked Emmy because, short of
the pearl-handled Derringer that she could wear
attached to her garter, she had no way to stop a man

such as Hank O'Shea. And truly, she did not think a gun as small as that would even slow him down. Not for long.

In a moment of true fear, she considered contacting Free Cyrus Franklin again. He'd spirited away Millie out from under Mistress's nose and away from the Jeweled Ladies. Once, at the dry-goods store where the Jewels did most of their shopping, Franklin had stopped her and, under the guise of kissing her hand, slipped her a note from Millie.

The note had been short, but happy. Millie was married to a rancher—a Civil War veteran who treated her well. She was mother to his son and expecting her first child. She was happy to be well and free of the Jeweled Ladies, all thanks to Free Cyrus.

The man had somehow come into money and he used it to help former slaves and veterans start new lives out west. Apparently, that included prostitutes. If anyone could get Emmy out of Brimstone quietly, it'd be Free Cyrus Franklin.

But Raymond's note stayed her hand. *All was well.* She trusted Raymond, even if she didn't trust Hank. Surely, if Raymond said so, things would turn out?

But she didn't hear anything else from him—or from Hank O'Shea. She entertained her callers and did her shopping and, in general, carried on as if nothing was amiss. It was easy enough to pretend.

Until Sunday, that was.

"Mr. O'Shea requests the pleasure of your company for tea in the parlor again," Mistress said from the doorway to Emmy's room. Today she was in a shimmering gold gown, as if dressed for the opera instead of visiting on a Sunday. "Shall I turn him away?"

72

Emmy's first reaction was to say *yes*, emphatically. But she hadn't heard from Raymond beyond that note and her curiosity got the better of her. "I can handle him."

"Do you know what he wants? I'm not running a tea house here," she said, sounding almost peevish about the fact. Emmy had to wonder if she was charging him for the tea—or her time—or if she was letting it play out.

"I'm still trying to understand his motives." And, specifically, whether they were true or not.

With a nod, Mistress turned to go. "Mistress? I think it shall take me quite some time to get into my gown. Perhaps you should keep Mr. O'Shea company?" In other words, would she do some digging for Emmy?

Mistress smiled wisely. "But of course. A fine looking man, Mr. O'Shea. I would be more than tempted to take him into my own bed."

Emmy schooled her features into amusement, but honestly, the thought bothered her. If Hank were charged with keeping Raymond's secrets, Mistress would be able to seduce them out of him.

Emmy did not rush. She only had one other day dress that did not project seduction—but Hank O'Shea wanted something from her. She may not have a lot of power, but she had some. She put on her richest gown, a heavy emerald green silk embroidered with black crystals around the bodice—with her one emerald necklace as a match. She'd display her assets and see if she could sway him, just as he'd tried to sway her with a promise of money and security.

She took extra time with her hair and dabbed her *eau de toilette* behind her ears. She was Emerald

73

Green. Men wanted to possess her and women wished, however secretly, that they could be her.

And she would not bend to his will. She owed him nothing.

She swanned down the stairs and then paused, for Mistress was indeed holding Hank in conversation.

"… Why is it that we do not see you here, Mr. O'Shea? A fine specimen such as yourself would be welcomed by my girls. I'm sure they wouldn't mind sharing you." Her voice dropped to a conspiratorial whisper. "Although I would keep you all to myself."

Emmy leaned closer to the doorway—as close as she could without actually sticking her head through the parlor door.

"Mistress, a woman of your many charms certainly wouldn't want to waste your time on a poor fellow like me."

Emmy almost snorted. He'd offered her a thousand dollars! That did not qualify as poor in her book—or Mistress's.

But she could tell from the delicate tinkling in Mistress's laugh that she was genuinely amused. "Oh, you are rich. And that accent? But you must tell me. If you don't come here, where do you go?"

"Ah—you have me wrong, Mistress. I am a paragon of virtue."

As Emmy rolled her eyes at *that* lie, Mistress replied easily, "Oh, I rather think you're not. I recognize a like-minded soul when I see one, Mr. O'Shea. For you and I—we do what needs to be done, do we not?"

"That, my dear lady, is true. However, I do not patronize whorehouses."

74

Emmy could see the look of disbelief that Mistress was no doubt giving him. It matched her own. Men had their weaknesses, all of them. And he was nothing but a man.

"But this is not a whorehouse, Mr. O'Shea," Mistress scolded him—but Emmy could tell that she was still smiling. *Flirting*.

"Indeed." He chuckled, and oddly, Emmy felt the noise in her chest. Her nipples tightened, which made her frown. She was not supposed to have such a reaction to him, of all people. "I will say this is the nicest bordello I've ever been in. I am most impressed by all you've accomplished, Mistress."

"But you just said you didn't patronize establishments such as mine." There was a hint of whine to her voice.

"Oh, I've been in many a whorehouse," he said affably, almost as if he were telling a joke. "But never as a patron."

Emmy's eyes went wide—had he just said *that*? Had she misheard him?

She must have. There was a moment of hushed tension that radiated out of the room before Hank added, "And I never did have a Mistress such as you. If I had... who knows?" She could imagine his innocent shrug. "Perhaps I would still be there. It would be hard to leave a place such as this." There was a pregnant pause. "But a gilded cage is still a cage, no?"

Emmy was impressed. Whether or not he spoke the truth remained to be seen—but he had managed to shock Mistress into silence.

But Emmy was shocked, too. Because if he had worked on his back—or his knees—then... then what

75

did that mean? That Raymond had a way of finding whores and soiled doves with some misguided belief that he had to save them from themselves? Although Hank O'Shea didn't need saving.

Not that the silence lasted. Mistress was far too quick for that. "You should come work for me, Mr. O'Shea," she cooed. "Together, we could run this town."

At that, Hank laughed. "You do tempt me. But you forget something." His voice lowered to that growl that made her traitorous nipples positively ache. "I already run this town, Emily."

Emmy gasped at the implicit threat. Which was a mistake because, seconds later, Hank said, "Perhaps you'd like to join us, Miss Green? I was just getting to know your Mistress better. I find I like her quite a bit."

"The feeling is mutual, I'm quite sure," Mistress said, her head bowed demurely as Emmy made her grand entrance. Mistress and Hank both stood and Emmy almost had to laugh as they both gave her a nearly identical nod of approval. "I shall leave you to your tea, Mr. O'Shea."

He bent low over her proffered hand. "The pleasure has been entirely mine, Mistress."

She beamed at him—and, for a second, Emmy thought she saw something more real in Mistress's face. Something that looked almost... lonely. "My door will always remain open to you, Mr. O'Shea."

Still bent over her hand, Hank's gaze cut to Emmy. "This will be my last visit to the Jeweled Ladies."

"My *private* door," Mistress added in a quiet voice.

In response, Hank pressed his lips to the back of her hand. Emmy swore she could feel the man's lips on her own hand, her own body, so potent was his kiss.

Emmy would not allow her body to react to Hank O'Shea. But as he aimed a heated glance at Mistress, it was clear that was going to be far easier said than done.

Blushing like an innocent schoolgirl, Mistress swept out of the room, leaving Emmy alone with this...

This *man*.

"I suppose you've come to offer me more money?" she said in her sweetest voice as she perched on the edge of the parlor chair.

"Of course not," he agreed far too readily.

Emmy busied herself pouring tea while she waited for him to get to the damn point. She was already on edge, but she wasn't about to let him see the effect he had on her. Finally, china cup in hand, she asked, "Then to what do I owe this 'pleasure'?"

He notched an eyebrow at the inflection she'd put into the word *pleasure*. "I come to ask a favor."

"Another one?" She sniffed delicately. "You ask for too much."

"You don't even know what I'm going to ask."

"I don't need to," she shot back. "I already know you're reprehensible and to think that I would want any favor you might wish to bestow upon me is sheer ego upon your part."

Any other man would have taken the insult to his pride as the slap it was intended to be. But Hank O'Shea was not any other man, for he smiled. A broad, warm thing that tried its hardest to coax a matching smile out of her.

She clamped her lips shut and refused to give him anything he wanted.

He leaned forward. "Ah, but what if the favor is something you want?" His gaze flitted around the room. "Respectability, comfort—love? What if I offered you a way out of this gilded cage?"

"You already offered that—or do you forget yourself, Mr. O'Shea? You and I both know that respectability can be bought." She slanted a sideways glance at him. "I cannot be bought."

"Your body?" His gaze raked over her body. "Aye. But your soul—ah, that is the ultimate prize, no?"

She could feel the flush where his eyes had lingered. "Perhaps you understand that better than I gave you credit for."

He showed no shame. "Perhaps."

"What I cannot guess at is why you would tell Mistress something so scandalous," she went on as conversationally as she could. "That gives her a hold over you."

"I consider it a gift," he said, sipping his tea. "Something to let her know that I pose no more threat to her than she does to me. But I wasn't telling her. I was telling you—and you were listening. We are safe with our secrets, are we not?"

She was not safe with him. He played too deep—and too well. "Are you going to get to the point today, Mr. O'Shea? My time is valuable."

He carefully set his cup down. "I want you to marry Raymond."

Her cup clattered on her saucer. "I beg your pardon?"

"You're loyal and true. There's not a woman alive who's better for him," he said with a small shrug.

"But..." she tried to find the right words. Was Raymond's lover—the man who tried to buy her off, for God's sake—asking her to marry Raymond? "But..."

"He has, of course, outlined the objections you both share about this. You're a soiled dove whose reputation would be a challenge for his political career and he cannot give you what you need to keep you happy within the marriage bed." He tossed these objections off as if they were trivial matters instead of insurmountable obstacles.

"Yes. And, as you might realize, I will not cuckold Raymond in marriage. I won't endanger him like that."

"Which is exactly why you need to marry him," he said with an odd glint in his eye. "I made him a promise. If I could find a solution that would leave both you and him satisfied..." his voice lingered over the word, sending skitters down Emmy's back, "*safely* satisfied, would you be willing to give up Emerald Green?" He leaned toward her and Emmy's breath caught in her throat. "Go back to being Emmeline McCartney in order to become Emmeline Dupree?" She couldn't answer. "He loves you, too, you know. It would kill him to see you marry anyone else."

She grasped at the few straws she had before her. "This town won't forget who I am."

He shrugged. "Maybe, maybe not. Money does talk, though. And you and I both know that Raymond won't be here long."

She tried to look bored—but that was hard to do around this man. "So what is this so-called 'solution' you think will solve our grand problem?"

There was that grin—he was a wolf and he had her

79

cornered. They both knew it. "On Tuesday, Raymond will come as he normally does. He'll arrange with Mistress for an additional night with you—Thursday, perhaps. Except that he'll request your presence at his home. We'll continue this discussion then."

"You'll be there?"

He didn't answer immediately. Instead, the seconds stretched and, in that pause, Emmy understood what he was about.

Him. Hank O'Shea was the solution. He would keep both Raymond and her.

"You're going to come out quite ahead on this, aren't you?" she murmured, no longer bothering to keep her shock to herself. Raymond's kisses, although well meaning, had left her cold.

And *cold* was not how Hank left her. Her body reacted to him whether she wanted it to or not.

"Raymond gets the woman he loves and he gets to be himself behind closed doors. You get power and respectability—and you get to keep the lifestyle you're accustomed to."

"And you?"

He sighed, a happy sound. "I won't suffer. You're no hardship, Emmy."

"You don't have leave to call me by that name."

"Not yet." He stood. "I look forward to seeing you again, Miss Green. But not here." He looked around the gilded, polished parlor. "No, not here." He placed his hat upon his head, a fine bowler that looked horribly out of place on his head. "Until Thursday?"

She didn't answer and, after a short pause, he nodded as if she had spoken.

And then he showed himself out.

Chapter Eight

The woman had spirit, Hank had to concede. Because she did not show up at Raymond's doorstep that Thursday. Neither did Raymond. Instead, they spent the night at the Jeweled Ladies while Hank cooled his heels in Raymond's parlor, his cock aching.

Because she was making something very clear to him—he did not have all the cards in this little game. He might have Raymond by the jewels—as he had this very afternoon—but she still held the man's heart.

By midnight, Hank couldn't take the pressure anymore. When Raymond slipped into the house under cover of darkness, he found Hank on the settee in the parlor, his cock in hand.

"Don't mind me," Raymond said, a hint of shock in his voice.

Hank deliberately stroked slowly, enjoying the way Raymond's eyes followed the movement. "You were supposed to bring her back here," he scolded, but his words came out strained as he fought for control.

"I don't know if you've noticed, but very few people tell Emmy what to do," Raymond replied. Hank expected him to take a step into the parlor—but he didn't. He leaned against the pocket doors and watched. "God, you're magnificent—you know that?"

"I try not to let it go to my—*ohh*—head," he finished, squeezing his tip and letting the pleasure race down his cock and tighten his jewels. "You could have a hand in this."

"I want to watch you," Raymond replied, his breath coming in short bursts.

"And—*unn*—Emmy?" He almost came at the thought of that fiery redhead's hands and mouth upon him. "Can you stand to watch her do this to me?"

Raymond was quiet as Hank stroked himself, up and down, slow and hard. He was still trying to get Raymond past his timidity and grip his cock like he meant it.

"I don't know," Raymond finally said, his voice a husky whisper. "I... I might get jealous of you. Jealous of her." He took a step into the room, then another. He was almost close enough for Hank to grab and haul down to his lips.

"Can you stand to see me kiss her, Raymond?" Because he imagined that there had been quite a little discussion back at the Jeweled Ladies tonight about whether they should stay there or come here—and Raymond hadn't insisted. He'd done as Emmy requested—because maybe he wasn't ready to share. "Can you stand to see me put my mouth on her, to suckle at her breast and put my cock in her pussy?"

"I've never seen her—her pussy," he said, swallowing nervously. Even that word sounded wrong in his mouth. Dirty, somehow.

Hank groaned again as he tried to fight his release. He was losing the battle. "You have to, if you want this to work. You *have* to share me with her. Or..."

"Or?"

"Or join us in bed." Raymond gasped but the image assembled itself like a picture in Hank's mind. Emmy's soft body laid out before him, open and wet and so, so pink, while Raymond knelt next to her, his cock in Hank's mouth. "I could fuck her while I suck you off, Raymond. I pump into her while you pump into my mouth—or you could fuck me, too, Raymond. Did you ever think—*uhh*!"

His spunk burst from his cock in an explosion of lust, coating his shirt. Ah, well. He collapsed back on the settee, panting hard. Then Raymond was upon him, straddling him. He grabbed Hank's hands and pinned him against the back of the settee. Hank could feel the heat from Raymond's cock burning through his pants and all he could wonder was, which part had turned him on the most?

"You're trying to shock me with your foul mouth," he growled.

"Is it working?" Hank let the man hold him down. Already, his cock was stirring again. "Because I think you need to be shocked, my beautiful man. Thoroughly and completely shocked—"

That was as far as he got before Raymond slammed his mouth over Hank's and then the two of them were tearing at their clothes and he was pushing Raymond on his back and sucking him off, hard and fast.

It was only when Raymond had cried out as his seed had spurted down Hank's throat for the second time that day and they lay still—having thoroughly desecrated the settee—that Raymond said, "I don't know how to fuck you. I mean, if it's different from what we've been doing."

"The things it does to me, to hear your proper mouth say such words," Hank growled, guiding the man's hand to his cock. "In time. It won't happen tonight. Not after *that*," he added, patting Raymond's sated cock.

"You really want to fuck Emmy?"

His cock twitched in Raymond's palm and the man tightened his grip. "God, yes. She's gorgeous," Hank said with a shudder. "Smart and quick, too."

Raymond was silent for a moment longer as he lazily stroked Hank. "Can this work? The three of us, that is?"

Hank shrugged. "It can, I suppose. I knew husbands and wives who were looking for a toy, back when I worked the streets. I had a few offers to join households on a more permanent basis."

"And you didn't?"

Hank knew Raymond was trying to understand how a boy on the streets would turn down room and board. "I couldn't. That gave them too much power, to put them in charge of my food and bed. I couldn't be dependent on them."

Raymond was silent.

They'd discussed this in theoretical terms—if he and Emmy married, they would live here—and Hank would move in. It would be portrayed as having all of Raymond's employees under his roof—a personnel move. Only the three of them would know the truth.

"You'd live with me. With Emmy and me."

"I would." He nuzzled against Raymond's neck. The man smelled of bay rum and hair tonic and sex, with a hint of something else—something lilac. *Emmy.* Emmy's scent was on him. The combination was heady.

"I'd be paying your salary for the work you do as assistant to the mayor."

"Aye."

Raymond pushed him back and stared him in the eyes. "You'd be dependent on me. Completely."

"Aye."

"Why would you do that?"

He touched his forehead to Raymond's. "You know why." When Raymond shook his head, Hank sighed. "I'm not your toy and you're not mine. This isn't just sex." It was something far bigger, far more satisfying.

Love. He'd never thought he would have love, be worthy of it. But Raymond was here now and Hank's feelings—well, they felt a lot like love.

"Ah," Raymond said, an exhalation on Hank's skin. "Come to bed, then. We still have time."

"Aye," Hank said, letting Raymond stand and then pulling him to his feet. "All the time in the world."

*

"Is he in there?" Emmy said as Raymond pulled the carriage to a halt in front of his house. She knew where he lived, of course. It was hard to miss the big Dupree mansion on the corner lot two blocks off Main Street. The house towered over the others and the newer money was always trying to out-build the Dupree mansion. But those fine houses were farther out of town. Raymond's house was a landmark.

"He is."

She eyed the dark windows nervously. As much as she tried, she was failing at not being nervous. This was nothing more than another evening, she tried to tell herself. She spent many a night in bed with men and, above all else, Raymond Dupree and Hank O'Shea were just men.

But that lie didn't work because Raymond, at least, was much more than a patron. She had not yet figured Hank out.

Raymond came around and held out a hand for her. "Nervous, darling?"

She tried to put on a smile, but Raymond knew her too well. "A little, I suppose. I would feel more comfortable in my room at the Jeweled Ladies." There, at least, she would have the familiar surroundings and the knowledge that Samuel and Mistress were but a shout away.

One of Mistress's rules was the Jewels had to stay in the brothel. She did not send girls out where she couldn't protect them, no matter the price offered. But Emmy had agreed to this and Mistress had relented.

Emmy was on her own here.

"You have nothing to fear," Raymond reassured her as he helped her down. "This is just... a test. Hank thinks this could be the solution but if not, it's..." he swallowed. "It'll be just fine."

Another lie. She and Raymond were not used to such lies and they both failed miserably at it. Still, though, she put on her placid face.

"If it does not work," Raymond said, his head bent close to her ear as they made the very public stroll up to his front door, "do not pretend. Promise me that. All I have ever asked is that you be honest with me."

She nodded. "I shall."

Raymond unlocked the huge front doors and led

her into the house. This was all real, she thought. The Jeweled Ladies was a fine house—but the Dupree mansion was something else entirely. Where the brothel was overdone and, past the parlor, sprawling and haphazard, this was subtle. The wealth here didn't have to shout like it did at the brothel. It was a quiet power, one that commanded respect without demanding it.

And this could all be hers, if only she enjoyed bedding Hank O'Shea.

Speak of the devil, he was standing in the dim parlor, a brandy snifter in his hand. His tie was gone, as was his jacket. Hank stood there in his waistcoat, his shirtsleeves rolled up to nearly his elbow.

And he was watching her.

"Miss Green," he said with a bow of his head.

"Emmy," she replied, not offering him her hand. "I think here, I am only Emmy." She couldn't be Emerald Green with Raymond, anyway, and she had promised honesty.

Raymond slipped her mink stole from her shoulders. As the fur skimmed over her bare arms, she shivered.

Hank saw that shiver. His eyes warmed. "Emmy," he said, his accent stroking over her name. "I am glad to see you again."

"Are you?"

He smirked. "Would you care for a drink? The brandy is excellent, but Raymond also has sherry." He motioned to the decanters set out on the low table before the settee. "He says you are partial to it."

"Sherry will be fine." A drink would settle her nerves.

Hank moved to pour her a glass and she looked for Raymond. He'd moved and was now sitting in a side chair before the fireplace. The room was dark and getting darker as dusk settled over them. "And you?" she asked Raymond, because Hank was acting more like her host than a guest.

"I'm fine," he assured her. And he did look perfectly at ease. "I'm here if you want me." In other words, she was on her own with Hank. "Emmy, darling, would you be comfortable if I lit a lamp and closed the drapes?"

She didn't want Hank sneaking up on her. If he were going to touch her—touch her more, that was— she wanted to see him coming. "You may, dear."

Hank didn't move while they waited. Instead, he handed her the glass of sherry. Moments later, light flickered and then caught as Raymond lit the hurricane lamp. He moved around Hank and Emmy as he went to pull the drapes. They were enclosed in a cocoon, a place out of time. The room felt warmer already, but she kept her eyes on Raymond.

When he had returned to his side chair, Hank took a step toward her and said, "Tell me about you and Raymond." His voice was close to her ear. Raymond gave her a little nod and, taking a steadying breath, she turned.

Hank stood, his brandy in his hand. It was tempting to down her sherry in one gulp, but she'd never been one to dull the senses. She swirled the amber liquid, breathing in the heady scent. "Hasn't he told you everything?"

"Aye—but men and women," he said with a smile that sent another flush of warmth through her body, "are a bit different, in my experience. So tell me about him."

She took a sip of the sherry and let it burn down her throat. "We undress each other. Like old married people. I undo his necktie and his buttons and he undoes mine and unlaces my corset."

Hank waved a hand over his front. "I already removed the tie. Sorry."

She gave him a dull look. "No, you're not."

He took her glass and set it down. Then stepped around her back. She felt his fingers find the small buttons and begin to work at them with ease. "Like this?"

"Yes." But that was all she said.

"What do you like about him?" Hank asked, his voice warm against her neck.

She let her eyes drift shut as the buttons gave, one by one. She tried to focus on Raymond, on his face, on the way his body felt when she lay curled up against him.

But that's not what swam before her eyes. Instead, she saw Hank, all callused hands and hot breath and calculating eyes. Her dress sagged a little and a rush of cool air kissed her nipples. "He's kind and warm and sweet and honest. He's everything a good man should be."

"Aye, on that we agree." Her dress gave and his fingers skimmed over her exposed shoulders before they moved down, pushing the dress forward so that it slid down her body.

She stepped out of the dress. "He's everything you're not." It was a rude thing to say, but the man was stripping her down, making a mockery of the special closeness she shared with Raymond.

Raymond chuckled from his seat.

89

"That he is," Hank said, his voice more hot that warm. "I am hard and rough. I can be crude. I lack morals or ethics. I do what needs to be done." She felt the laces on her corset give and then he was pulling them loose. Her bosom released and she exhaled in relief. "What's more, Raymond likes me that way."

His lips brushed over her shoulder. Heat rushed from where he touched her and pooled lower in her body. "Does he?"

"I do," Raymond said and she heard something that she didn't recognize in his voice. Heat. *Desire.*

She'd never been able to bring out that desire in him. Not on her own. But Hank brought it out in Raymond effortlessly. Damn him, he could bring it out in her, too.

"Pick up her dress," Raymond said, his voice tight with want. "Lay it out so it doesn't wrinkle."

She expected Hank to hesitate at this direct order—but he didn't. He snatched her very best dress off the ground and shook it out.

"As you can see, Raymond is a perfect gentleman," she said to Hank as she turned to face him. "A *perfect* gentleman." She stood in her sheer shift—her very best one that had cost her over twenty dollars—and her loosened corset. Underneath that were her garters and stockings.

"No drawers?" Hank asked, his eyes lingering on where the vee of her legs met.

"What kind of a whore do you take me for?" she asked in mock indignity.

"One of the very finest," he replied, which oddly made her feel better—more like the way they sparred in the parlor at the Jeweled Ladies.

"Too good for the likes of you."

In reply, Hank leaned toward her, his gaze raking over her body. He unfastened the busks on her corset but instead of letting it fall, he pulled it away and draped it over the back of the settee. "Does Raymond get to see you like this?"

She lifted a shoulder. "Not that he looks, but yes. He gets me like this."

"You are a vision, Emmy."

She rolled her eyes. "Sir, you have—thus far—proven to be different from any other man of my acquaintance. Don't start spouting the same tired platitudes now. It's beneath you."

Hank glanced over her shoulder, where Raymond was laughing. "Oh, I do like her."

"As do I," Raymond agreed.

"Do you tell her how beautiful she is, Raymond?"

"All the time," he said in all earnestness.

Emmy did not like that they would discuss her as if she weren't here. "He does."

"Let me hear."

Hank stood to the side as Raymond joined them. As was their custom, Emmy extended her hand to him. He smiled, his eyes twinkling. "My darling Miss Green, your beauty remains unsurpassed," he said loftily.

Hank snorted and Emmy glared at him. "What? That was a perfectly lovely compliment."

Hank shook his head. "Raymond, you have *so* much to learn if you're going to marry this woman." Raymond looked chastened and she didn't want that. But before she could defend him, Hank went on, "You compliment her as if she were a painting, a fine painting hanging on a wall—not a living, breathing woman who moves under you in bed. No one will believe you lust after her with your soul if that's how you treat her in public."

"Oh?" Emmy shot at him, unable to rein in her mouth. "And how would you advise him to treat me? Paw at me like a piece of meat?" She scoffed. "I get quite enough of that."

Hank turned his attention to her. "You have luscious tits, you know that?"

"He says that in public and I'll slap him."

Hank ignored her. Instead, he glanced at Raymond and nodded toward Emmy's bosom. "When you compliment her dress, what you're really saying is that her tits are luscious."

Raymond looked worried. "I am?"

"Watch," Hank said. He lifted Emmy's hand in his and, reluctantly, she let him. Then, somewhat more obviously than he had in the parlor at the Jeweled Ladies, he let his gaze work over her body. He lifted her hand to his lips and, just before he kissed the back of her hand, he said, "My dearest Emmeline, that dress does not do you justice."

The compliment itself wasn't any better than what Raymond had said—but the way Hank said it was. His voice was all warmth and barely contained sex and intoxication. She was *intoxicated*. "Oh," she said, feeling her cheeks pink with a blush that might've been virginal on an actual virgin.

"Ah, you see?" Hank went on, his gaze never leaving her face. "Emmy heard the difference. The words don't matter, Raymond. But if you want people to believe you bed this woman and that this woman has forsaken all others for you—you must learn to say that with every action, every touch, every single glance."

Emmy didn't want to tell Hank that he was right about that—so she said nothing. Then he finally pressed his lips to the back of her hand. Heat— traitorous heat—sparked through her and she shivered.

"You promised, Hank."

"What?" She looked back at Raymond. "What did he promise?"

"That I would not use you ill, Emmy," Hank replied. She turned back to him, expecting to see that calculating smile working over his features.

But it wasn't there. In its place was an earnestness that seemed out of place on his face.

"That's rich, coming from you," she said.

He shrugged. "Are you going to undo my buttons?"

"No. I only do that for men I love. And I've made no such promises," she told him. "The only promise I've made to Raymond is to be honest. So this is my honest opinion of you, Hank O'Shea. I don't like you. You're conniving and underhanded and untrustworthy."

As she spoke, he began to undo the buttons on his waistcoat and then his shirt. "And?"

"And Raymond has put his faith in you and I cannot see why." But even as she said it, her eyes followed his hands as he pulled the tails of his shirt from his trousers. He stripped the shirt and waistcoat off together instead of one at a time. Then he shucked his undershirt.

She sucked in a breath. It wasn't a surprise, that he looked like that. But she hadn't been prepared for the magnitude of his muscles.

He noticed her staring and paused, the muscles across his chest tightening. "And?" he said, his voice low and dangerous.

93

"That's all. I don't like you."

He wagged a finger at her. "You're lying, Emmy. That's not all."

"Yes," she said, her cheeks warming with the lie—warming as his fingers moved to the buttons on his trousers. "There's nothing else."

"There is." He kicked out of the trousers and then undid the drawstring on his drawers. His clothes were of good quality and his underclothes were clean and in good repair.

And then the drawers were gone and Hank O'Shea stood before her, completely naked—and hard. "There's this. You may not like me, but you react to me. I've seen it from the very first. And," he added, waving his hand over his cock, "I react to you."

Oh, his cock—it was thick, jutting out from a thatch of unruly black hair. But he also had a decent length to him. Hard and rough and crude—his cock fit him perfectly. And she had no doubts that he knew how to use that tool to the very best advantage.

Just the thought of that magnificent cock sliding between her thighs, into her pussy—she got wet at the thought.

Damn him, he was right. She didn't have to like him to fuck him—and he didn't have to like her to bring her to her crisis.

Behind her, Raymond sighed in satisfaction. "It provokes quite a reaction in me, too."

Emmy laughed in spite of herself. "Impressive."

He smirked even as his cock twitched. "Ah, Emmy, don't spout the same tired platitudes you say to every man who takes to your bed. It's beneath you."

"Then what shall I tell you?"

He considered this for a while. "The truth. What do you want from me?"

She lowered her gaze to his tool again.

"In words, sweetling," Hank said, the brogue of his voice thick. "So we all know."

"I want..." She swallowed, uncharacteristically nervous again. "I want to break. I want to come apart. And not just once or twice—I want satisfaction regularly. Nightly, even."

Hank's brow furrowed with concern, but it was Raymond who spoke next. "Do you not get that now?"

She laughed, a mirthless tone. "I don't know if you can understand but," she added, turning back to Hank, "you will. So many men poke me with their staffs. They thrust and grunt and I make a great noise about how good they are, how much they fill me."

"They pay you for that," Hank said, nodding in sympathy.

"I am a fine whore," she agreed, "but one of the best actresses of my age. And they love me for it. They fall in love with me, with what they think they can give me. But I'm not going to be the butcher's wife or marry the hotelier, not when neither man has any clue about how to please me. I want pleasure."

"Have you ever come apart?" Hank asked, his tone careful.

She shrugged. "It happens. Sometimes, a man surprises me. Sometimes I manage to bring myself to completion—but so often, I simply don't have the energy. There is so much sex and so few orgasms that... that sometimes, I do not see the point in it."

This admission surprised Raymond, who made concerned noises behind her. Hank's thick black eyebrows rose mightily. But no one in the room was more surprised than Emmy herself.

When was the last time she'd broken? It had been... a while. A long while. Before Raymond had started coming to her. She vaguely remembered a man, an older man who was on his way to Mexico. Perhaps he was running from the law or... she didn't know. He hadn't looked like anything special—she remembered he'd had all his teeth—but instead of just flipping up her skirts and fumbling out of his pants, he'd taken his time with her. He'd stroked and fondled her and...

And she had not had to act. Not that night. But, sadly, her unnamed patron had never been seen again.

She stared openly at Hank's cock. Size, she had learned, did not mean everything. Still, she did not want to act tonight.

"I will make you break, sweetling," Hank promised her, his voice too tender by half.

Her eyes burned, but rather than dignify that with a response, she turned to Raymond. The man was rubbing at his cock through his pants in an absentminded way as he watched the little show she and Hank put on for him. "And you're okay with this, dear? You can watch him fuck me like the whore I really am?"

Raymond closed the distance between them. He put his hands on her shoulders and touched his forehead down to hers. "I... I don't know. But I want you to be happy and I know you need that," he said, motioning back toward Hank's cock, "and I know I cannot give that to you. I love you both and if I have to share you with each other to make sure everyone's satisfied, then I shall."

She felt Hank step in close behind her, and then his hand settled around her waist. Lord, but the man ran hot. Raymond's hands were smooth and cool against her shoulders—but Hank's hands were searing her skin underneath the sheer fabric of her shift.

And then his cock bumped against her hip and everything got so much hotter. She reached behind her and encircled Hank's cock with her fingers. "Is this for me or for Raymond?" she asked as she pulled on him.

"Right now," he breathed in her ear, his hands sliding forward over the shift until he'd cupped her sex in his hand, "you're the one who's undressed."

"Such sweet nothings," she scoffed. Or she tried to scoff, but just at that second, Hank's fingers parted her folds and he pressed against her very sex with the expert precision of a man who knew exactly what he was doing. Emmy gasped, and without her permission, her hips shifted, grinding down onto his hand.

"Look at how you respond, sweetling. Raymond, do you see?"

Emmy lifted her gaze to Raymond's face. He was studying her, concern and hope all mixing together in his eyes. Hank began to rub small circles on her flesh, the silk of her shift sliding over her. Her eyes tried to roll back in her head, but she held Raymond's gaze.

"Does it feel good?" Raymond whispered.

"Does it?" Hank echoed, his other hand sliding up to her breast. He pinched her nipple between his fingers and gave a tug that she mirrored with her grip on his cock. "Damn, Emmy—because you feel good."

"Hush," Raymond said, his gaze still locked on hers and Hank toyed with her body. "Is it all right, darling?"

97

Emmy's mouth opened but nothing came out. Hank gave her pussy a little tap—not a smack, nothing hard—but the sensation shot through her like a cannon ball and she moaned. With her free hand, she clutched at Raymond's shirt in an effort to keep her legs under her.

"Emmy?" he asked worriedly. "All right?"

"Yes," she gasped as she leaned her head against Raymond's shoulder. "He's—he's very skilled."

"I'm out of practice," Hank murmured behind her. "As I told Raymond, when I left Boston, I vowed to keep out of anyone's bed. It's been years. Well," he added with a chuckle as he tweaked her nipple again, "it had been, until a few weeks ago." She arched her back and suddenly, Hank was carrying her weight in his arms. "Bed or settee?"

She looked at Raymond, who only said, "You decide."

She didn't like how cool Hank still sounded as he was driving her mad. She needed room to work because he might make her shatter, but by God, she was going to destroy his control, too. He would not leave with the upper hand. They would part as equals or they would not meet again.

"Bed," she said decisively.

Chapter Nine

L ead on, Raymond." As he spoke, Hank swept her into his arms. While Raymond picked up the lamp, Hank asked, "Is there anything that you will refuse?"

She held herself tense for a moment, but he was warm and it was quite considerate of him to ask. "I do not like it when men try to take my other hole."

She shouldn't have been surprised when Hank nodded. "Completely understood. Anything else?"

"I do not enjoy being tied down." The helplessness that men wanted her to feel when they tried that—it wasn't erotic. It was scary. A whore's life was a dangerous one but the only time she'd ever truly feared for her life was the one time she'd let a man tie her to the bedpost. He'd promised a little fun, something to enhance her pleasure and his. But once she'd been secured, he'd turned into a monster.

Never again. She'd already put herself at their mercy by taking their money and taking off her clothes. She didn't want to give up what was left of her control.

"Pity, that," Hank said, warm humor in his voice. "I think Raymond might like tying me to the bedpost one night."

Her head popped up and she stared at him. "Really?"

"Really?" Raymond echoed as he reached the top of the stairs and paused.

"Indeed. He's held me down several times when he's crazed with lust. I think he might enjoy it."

"And you? Would you enjoy it?" Because she could not imagine that this man would submit so willingly. *He* pulled the strings. *He* did the things Raymond couldn't. He was *not* submissive.

Hank chuckled. "I enjoy giving myself to him. You must believe that, Emmy."

In unison, they turned to look at Raymond, who seemed lost in thought. Then he shook his head. "Let us not muddle the issue. Tying you down is separate from what happens with Emmy."

Emmy felt a grin curve up the corners of her lips. She glanced up at Hank and saw him smiling down at her. They understood what Raymond had just said. There was a very good chance that Raymond would like to try that—and maybe even soon.

"This way," Raymond said, leading the way to the front of the house. "The master bedroom," he said, pushing open the door and setting the lamp down at a table by the bedside.

Emmy looked around at the room. It spoke of Raymond to her with the heavy velvet drapes, a deep shade of blue, and in the massive four-poster bed hung with matching blue bed curtains. The wardrobe was twice the size of hers—everything in the room made her feel small.

Or maybe that was the man who was tenderly laying her out on the bed. He'd carried her through the length of the house as if she weighed nothing, his rippling muscles moving against her, his thick cock jutting against her bottom. Hank took up so much room that everything felt smaller in his presence. Including her.

She watched all those muscles as Hank stood before her. He grasped the hem of her shift and gently pulled it over her head. Then he went to work on her garters and stockings, rolling them down.

Then she was stripped. Nothing lay between her and him—or Raymond. She looked around until she found him, sitting in another side chair near the fireplace. His face was in shadows, but she could tell from his posture that he was watching them intently. He gave her a little nod. *Go on.*

He loved Emmy's heart and Hank's body. Could she forge the same compromise?

"And you?" she asked, turning her attention back to Hank. "Anything that you don't want me to do?"

He knelt onto the bed, causing her to scoot toward the middle. "Hmm," he said, glancing over his shoulder to where Raymond sat. He adjusted his position—giving Raymond a better view, no doubt. "I like it rougher. But please, do leave my ears alone. No tongues or pulling there."

What an odd request. "Consider it done. Shall we begin?"

She expected him to climb on top of her and start pounding away—but he didn't. Instead, he lay out along side of her and began skimming his hands from her hip to her breast and back. "We've already begun, sweetling. You deserve much more than a quick fuck."

Her body thrummed at his words and she was

101

tired of fighting it. He was going to have her—that was a forgone conclusion at this point. But, for the first time, she considered the possibility that he was going to make it good. He wasn't just going to be good—although he probably was. He was going to take the time and make sure she shattered.

She achieved her crisis *so* rarely. Men weren't paying for her to get off—they were there solely to come inside of her. Or, in some cases, on her. And that was not romantic. She grabbed at her pleasure where she could, but it was always such a fleeting thing, dancing at the edge of a place where she could clamp down on it until it left her destroyed. It was never something she could hold onto. But she wanted to. Oh, how she wanted to.

If he were truly going to put her first...

"Can I touch you?" she asked, feeling oddly timid about it. But then, this wasn't a performance and she wasn't a mere receptacle for spunk.

He stilled and she saw his eyes grow dark. "Aye, I wish you would."

She started at his shoulders and let her hands drift over his chest. "You're hot," she said.

His hand stroked over her belly as he bent his head and pressed a kiss to her shoulder. "Aye, the cold doesn't touch me. Kept me alive more than once."

"I..." she swallowed. "I like your voice," she admitted as she felt his thick arms. His fingers weren't terribly long—blunt. That was how she'd describe them. They didn't look like the hands of a man who wrote for a living. "It reminds me of home."

"Looking at you," he whispered against her skin, "I feel the same." Then his hand dipped lower, stroking over the hair that covered her sex as his teeth skimmed over her skin. She gasped when his fingers delved deeper. "Sweet Emmy, what do you taste like?" he asked as he pushed a finger inside of her. Then he withdrew it and sucked the digit into his mouth. "Ah— sweet," he said, slipping the moist finger back among her folds and rubbing those languorous circles again.

He wasn't fighting fair, so she retaliated the only way she knew how. She took his member in hand and began slow, unhurried strokes.

God help her, he did run hot. He was smooth under her fingers, his hips thrusting forward at her touch ever so slightly.

"Harder, lass," Hank whispered. "Rough. I like it rough."

She squeezed and twisted her hands over his member and a low groan issued from his chest. There. That was better. He may be fingering her, but she had him in her thrall as well. And if he liked it rough?

She rolled into him and bit him on the chest. Not hard enough to draw blood, but enough to mark his skin temporarily. He shuddered and pulled her on top of him. "Aye, woman," he growled, tweaking at her nipples while she ground against his length. "Let me give you what you want." His hips flexed underneath her, sliding his member along the folds of her pussy. "Tell me how to make you come undone."

She notched an eyebrow at him in challenge. "Anything?"

"What you want. Whatever you want."

Emmy glanced over her shoulder at Raymond. He was leaning forward, his elbows on his knees and his hands clasped in what looked like prayer. He'd lost his jacket at some point and was in his shirtsleeves. "Anything I want?"

"Take him," Raymond whispered in a shaky voice. "I... I want to see you two together." He swallowed. "Fuck for me."

"Raymond, such language," she teased as she scooted her hips forward and reached down behind her to cup Hank's jewels. "I didn't know you capable of it."

Raymond exhaled heavily as she fondled Hank—who, for his part, still had a grip on her nipples. He pulled and pinched, sending waves of pleasure that rode the ragged edge of pain throughout her body. "He likes it," Raymond whispered. "When I say such foul things."

"Aye," Hank said, writhing beneath her. "Such dirty words from such a sweet mouth. Makes me want to fuck him, too."

She turned back to Hank. "Should he join us?"

But Hank just shook his head. "No. Not this time. This is for you and I to try. If we like each other well enough to keep at it, then he can join us."

"Tell her," Raymond got out in a strangled voice. "Tell her what you said you'd do to us."

"Tell me," Emmy said, raking her nails down Hank's chest until she got to his flat nipple. Then she twisted it.

"Oh, aye," he groaned again. Her nipples suffered so wonderfully under his touch. "I'd lay you out and fuck you so hard, Emmy—and while I did, I'd suck Raymond off. I'd pump you full of seed while he spurted down my throat and I'd suck him dry, every last drop."

Raymond muttered, "Fuck," softly behind her, but her attention was on Hank.

"Is that all?" She gave his jewels another squeeze before relinquishing her hold on him and shifting back so that his throbbing member was rubbing along her pussy again. "Surely a man of your experience has other options."

"He's not ready yet." As he said it, Hank let go of her left breast and shoved his thumb into her curls. He pressed against her sex, making her gasp. With a wicked grin, he pulled himself up so that his mouth could settle on her breast. "He's still learning how to please a man in bed—and how to take his pleasure like a man."

"What have you—oh!" Hank's lips closed around her nipple and he began to suckle her in time with the pressure of his thumb on her sex. "What have you taught him?"

"How to suck, how to be sucked. He's good at it," Hank said in between suckling and biting at her breast. "Watching his sweet mouth take me in—God. *God.*"

Emmy drove her fingers into his mass of black hair and tilted his head up. "Don't you dare spend without making me break first."

Behind them, Raymond groaned.

"You see?" Hank said—but not to her. "See how she takes control? She how she tells me what I must and must not do?" When Raymond didn't reply, Hank said more sharply, "Raymond, are you learning?"

"I have never been this hard," he panted from the side chair.

"Take yourself in hand, man," Hank said, which made Emmy smile. Then he moved, flipping her onto her back. "We haven't even gotten to the part where I tell her how I'm going to bend you over and grease your hole up and push a finger into you, then two." As he said this, he pushed a finger back into Emmy's pussy, then a second. Her muscles clenched around him. The corner of his mouth curved up in a knowing smile. "Aye, like that, sweetling. And when you're nice and ready, Raymond, I'm going to put my cock in your ass. And while I do that, I'll reach around front and stroke you off until you scream. Because you *will* scream."

"Oh, God," Raymond moaned. She heard the sound of skin moving on skin as he did what Hank told him to.

The image was so sinful—but Emmy's curiosity was too much. "Is that all you'll teach him, then?"

"No. God, no. Because I want him to do the same thing to me. Except I want to be buried in your pussy when he fucks my hole."

But he still was only stroking his calloused fingers into her and it wasn't enough. The spasms of pleasure were lovely—but not everything. She wanted more. She wanted complete, mindless bliss that drove her out of her mind.

She dug her nails into his back. "Don't get ahead of yourself, sir. You have to make sure I'm well and properly fucked before you get to take both of us at the same time and, as of right now, I don't consider myself fucked at all, much less well."

He paused for a cruel second, meeting her challenge head on. Then his fingers inside of her twisted and he made a motion and hit a spot that had only been touched once or twice before. Emmy's shoulders came off the bed as the pleasure coursed through her body.

"Look at you," Hank said, his voice low as he lowered his mouth to her nipple again. "All those men and no one ever does right by you."

She was panting now, shamelessly panting as her hips writhed underneath him. "Hank," she moaned—but that was all she was capable of saying. No smart replies, no scolding nags—all she could say was his name.

Then he pulled away entirely, leaning over her to the bedside table. There he grabbed a small wooden box and opened it. Emmy watched in amusement as he pulled out the rubber. "Ever used one of these before?"

"Sheepskin, yes—Mistress requires we use something," she said—but this was different. It was smooth and—yes—rubbery as he rolled it onto his member. "Very... sleek," she noted.

He grinned as he grabbed her by the hips and positioned her where he wanted her. Then the head of his thick cock was against her pussy. She pulsed around him, needing him inside of her. Needing the release that was in his hands.

"So wet for me, sweetling," he said through clenched teeth.

"I don't like you," she reminded him in a desperate attempt to keep control over this situation. "So you better make this good. I have much to compare you to."

There—there was that grin, that of the wolf having finally cornered his prey. He flexed his hips and, meeting no resistance, grabbed her hips and slammed himself into her.

Emmy gasped as he filled her. "Good start," she struggled to say in a normal voice—but she failed. "Go on."

"Oh, you're a challenge, woman. And I do love meeting a challenge."

Hank fell upon her. He kept himself propped up on one arm so that he could play with her breasts with the other hand—and through it all, he kept a steady pace of thrust after thrust. "Meet me," he whispered in her ear.

So she wrapped her legs around his waist and lifted her hips in time with each of his thrusts and he fucked her. His pace was unhurried because he wasn't paying by the minute. Instead of pawing at her, he tweaked and pulled, finding the right amount of pressure that made her writhe and pant.

"Emmy," he panted in her ear. "God, woman, a man could get lost in you." Then he did something he hadn't yet done.

He kissed her. His whiskers scraped over her lips and then he settled himself more firmly against her. And the difference between the way Hank kissed her and the way Raymond had kissed her could not have been more obvious.

Hank filled her, surrounded her—he worshipped at her body with his own. Hank was hot and hard with all that brute strength kept barely in check.

And she responded. Oh, Lord—she responded. She lost herself in the pull and thrust of his body into hers. She met him, stroke for stroke, equals on the field. She kissed him back—which was not something she did a great deal of. But she gave him her mouth and feasted on his lips.

She gave him what he wanted, too. She dragged her nails over his back, bit his lips and sank her teeth into his shoulder. And for each cruelty, she was rewarded with a low, muttered curse, his arms shaking and his eyes rolling up into his head.

Then she was, once again, standing at the edge of her crisis, so close to it she could almost touch it. But it hovered just out of reach, a fog that wasn't solid enough to grasp.

"More," she begged. "Please, please—more." Because this was good—but she wasn't going to give herself over to anything less that great.

Hank grunted and shifted so that her knees were tucked under his arms. Then he fell upon her again, driving harder and deeper and hitting that place inside of her that cried out with joy at the attention.

She whipped her head from side to side, climbing higher and higher. She couldn't reach his back at this angle, so she attacked his nipples with her fingernails, tormenting him until he was shouting, "Fuck, woman!" over and over again.

It was only then that she became aware that Raymond had moved. He stood beside the bed now, his member in his hand and a look of utter debauchery on his face. When he caught her gaze, he smiled.

He was happy. This hadn't disgusted him, watching Hank take her. Raymond liked it. For all his sweetness and tenderness, Raymond Dupree was just as wicked as they were.

And they were all going to be *very* wicked—together.

Raymond looked over them and, shuddering into his own hand, said one word as he began to spill over the bedclothes, over Hank's thigh, over Emmy's side.

"*Mine.*"

Emmy pulled Hank down to her lips and shattered

as he kissed her. Seconds later, Hank followed her over the edge, shuddering into her with a furious thrust that set off a second wave of pleasure through her body.

Then they collapsed into each other, both panting and shaking. Hank weighed a bloody ton, but she didn't mind. "That was intense," she murmured, flinging her hand out to the side.

Raymond sat on the bed and took her hand in hers. "A good intense?"

Hank rolled to the side and, with one of his massive hands, pulled Raymond down on the bed so that, fully clothed, he was nestled between Hank and Emmy. Emmy happily curled into his side and Hank propped himself up on his elbow, only to lean down and kiss Raymond with all the fervor he'd kissed Emmy. She watched, still curious about this, about how they worked. But it was not bad because it was Raymond and she knew now that Hank would do anything to make him happy.

"Aye," he said, pulling away and cupping Raymond's face. "The best kind of intense." He reached across Raymond's chest to stroke her cheek. "And you?" he asked as he touched her.

"Yes, Emmy—please," Raymond whispered and she knew that his happiness rested on her shoulders. On her being his—and on him sharing Hank with her.

This was madness, of that there was little doubt. Complete and utter madness to give up the security of the Jeweled Ladies and enter into this arrangement with them. One night was bliss and perhaps more nights would be better, with Raymond taking his pleasure while Hank gave it to her.

But was that enough?

She could say *no*. She knew Raymond would button her back into her gown and deposit her back at the Jeweled Ladies and she could go on as she had before—selling comfort to men one hour at a time and rarely getting to take her own, hoping not to get the clap or with child, hoping that her patrons would treat her kindly as she lost her youth and beauty. Hoping she could hold on long enough to inherit the Jeweled Ladies from Mistress.

Really, was it much of a question?

She kissed Raymond's cheek and then shot a stern look at Hank. "It's possible that I might *learn* to like you," she conceded, but she couldn't keep the smile off her face as she said it.

Raymond gave a little shout of happiness. "Will you marry me, then?" And for all his foul words and wickedness that lurked just beneath the surface, he looked impossibly innocent and hopeful as he asked it.

"And will you have me?" Hank asked, nowhere near innocent, but still with hope at the corners of his eyes.

"Yes."

Raymond began to laugh with joy and Hank grinned, making him look far younger than Emmy had ever seen him. "Then we best make some plans," Hank said.

Plans. For a new life as a new wife.

Anything was possible, it seemed.

Mrs. Raymond Dupree.

She would be his during the daylight, but theirs after dark.

Chapter Ten

A nd so it was that the three of them decided upon a set of rules.

Firstly, Tuesday nights would remain Raymond and Emmy's. They needed to maintain the same closeness they had at the Jeweled Ladies if they wanted to preserve the illusion of marriage. Ancillary to that was the fact that Hank would absolutely not be in the house Tuesday nights. He would go out to the saloons and play cards and generally be far, far away from Raymond and Emmy while they cuddled in bed as the old married couple they soon would be.

Secondly, Emmy would leave the Jeweled Ladies as soon as she could. Hank was charged with finding her a respectable room in a respectable house to begin the rehabilitation of her reputation. She would leave Emerald Green behind and resume life as Emmeline McCartney.

Thirdly, she and Raymond would marry after a respectable courting period of three months. They all agreed that to some people—especially Judge Hobson—her reputation was incapable of being salvaged. But Emmy argued that if she went directly from the brothel to the chapel to Raymond's bed, it would be too shocking by half for the town. Three months gave Emmy the chance to prove that she had left her whorish ways behind and was devoted to Raymond. Plus, Raymond was due for reelection in two and a half months. Emmy didn't want to damage his odds, so she agreed that the wedding should wait until after the election.

Which meant two things.

Chaperones and chastity.

For three months, she was to be constantly supervised. She had to put on the performance of her lifetime and convince the entire town that she no longer spread her legs for money. She would begin to attend church on Raymond's arm every Sunday. She would be delicate and graceful and at no time would words like 'fuck' cross her lips in any company. During such time, she would acquire a wardrobe more befitting of a mayor's wife than of a whore. Raymond would pay for it, of course. Her trousseau would be part of the wedding, it was understood.

She would also adopt a pet cause, something good for the community. Perhaps she could fund a window in Raymond's church or buy new slates for the schoolchildren. Something that would be generous and valued by the finer folks of Brimstone, so that eventually, she would be valued by them, too.

Emmy understood the need for these rules but she chafed at the fact that Raymond and Hank could more or less continue on as they had been while she had to be 'rehabilitated.'

There were other rules. Hank would move into Raymond's house. They were going to make up some story about how Raymond needed to have his right-hand man by his side for planning night and day.

113

During the day, in public, Emmy was to treat Hank with cold indifference or even derision. Hank was to be seen as an underling and nothing more.

And, after a suitable period of time, they would discuss when they would start a family. This was a cause of some concern for Emmy because she and Raymond were fair and light and Hank was... not. A group of black-haired children would so very obviously be Hank's children, not Raymond's. But Raymond showed her a miniature portrait of his mother on her wedding day—and the woman had raven-black hair. So, he argued, if Emmy had a baby with black hair, they would say that it was his mother's hair coming through. The children would call Hank *Uncle*, but the three of them would raise the children together.

Beyond that, each promised the others that they would be honest. There were bound to be problems— especially for Raymond, who had both never lived with a lover and had, by and large, been alone for years. Sharing a home and a life with any one partner would be a challenge. Sharing it with two?

And finally, just as there were at the Jeweled Ladies, in bed there would be rules. Emmy wanted no part of any bindings; Hank and Raymond could do that on their own, if they so desired. No one would touch Hank's ears and Raymond would never be asked to do anything more than kiss or cuddle with Emmy. Emmy insisted that the two of them stop sucking each other off at the office. When they grumbled, she firstly pointed out that there was far too much risk of discovery, and more importantly, she was being asked to be completely celibate for three long, dull months.

They could at least keep their trousers fastened until they went home, for God's sake.

At that, neither Hank nor Raymond thought it wise to argue with her.

So things were, by and large, settled. Except for one very important thing.

"Mistress?" Emmy asked, knocking on the door to Mistress's office early Monday morning, after all the plans had been set in motion and she was confident of her decision to accept Raymond and Hank. "May I speak to you?"

A ripple of tension moved down Mistress's shoulders before she lifted her head from her ledgers and beamed a welcoming smile at Emmy. "Of course, my dear. Do come in and have a seat."

Emmy closed the door behind her. Mistress's office was on the second floor of the house, right over the formal parlor. It had good afternoon light, but was otherwise sparsely decorated. None of the finery of the parlor was visible here because this room, above and beyond any other room in the Jeweled Ladies brothel, was strictly forbidden to patrons.

Instead, everything was spare and well-made. The rug was an older one that had been in the parlor when Emmy had first come here, but aside from the drapes, it was the only decoration. Not even a painting graced the walls—only shelves with ledgers and books. Mistress had her desk arranged so that she had a view of the street and could see who was coming and going from the Jeweled Ladies.

Emmy did not sit. She was in no mood to be still.

This should not have been a problem. For heaven's sake, she had just agreed to marry one man, sleep with another and go to church every single Sunday—not to mention the three months of keeping no company but her own at night. Telling Mistress she was leaving was the least shocking of any of these decisions, frankly.

So why was Emmy so worried?

Mistress looked up at her. Emmy tried to smile, but it was almost as if she could no longer pretend.

Mistress noticed immediately. Her delicate nostrils flared and she carefully closed her ledger book. "Are you sure you want to do this, Emmy?"

It had been so long since Mistress had uttered a girl's name—any girl's name—instead of a gem that it momentarily stunned Emmy. "I do."

Mistress closed her eyes, as if she could ignore what was coming. "But to tie yourself to one man? Are you sure that will be enough for you? He won't tolerate being cuckolded, you know that."

Two men, she thought, struggling to keep the smile off her face. Raymond and Hank. It was more than enough for any one woman to manage. "I am capable of fidelity. He is worth it."

Mistress's eyelids flew open and she eyed Emmy closely. "Ah, but is he? We know men, you and I. How many married men come through our doors, because their wives cannot meet their needs? How many married men crave the variety that we offer them? Men are changeable creatures, dear. You know that as well as I do. Changeable, faithless—untrue. Untrue to all but themselves." There was a sadness in her voice, and not for the first time, Emmy wondered how Mistress had come to this place in her life and who she'd been when she'd been Emily.

116

"How many men would risk their political careers on a whore?" Emmy replied as calmly as she could. Because Mistress's concerns were valid—twice over. She had to ask for all of that from both Raymond and from Hank. "But I'm not one, not to him. This is my one chance, Mistress."

She scoffed. "You have had other proposals before. I have no doubt you will have other proposals again. And besides—you have always said no, dear. I..." her voice cracked and she paused, regaining control over her emotions. "I cannot keep doing this. Not forever. I had hoped that you would take my place. You would have all the power you want, all the freedom you want. You could have everything, Emmy."

"Everything except love."

She expected Mistress to roll her eyes at that, but to her surprise, the older woman didn't. Instead, she just looked... sad. Hopelessly sad and alone and every one of her many years. "Do you really think love is worth it?"

At that, Emmy did sit. She reached over the desk and took one of Mistress's hands in hers. "Mistress— Emily," she said softly.

"Don't try that, my dear," Mistress said sharply— but she didn't pull away.

"Haven't you ever wanted something more than this?" Emmy asked, not knowing what the answer would be. "A home, a family?"

Mistress shook her head. "You—all you girls— you are my family. And I had hoped that I was yours, too. I have tried..." Her gaze hardened and she did pull her hand back. "Remember when I found you, Emmy?

117

No more than sixteen, bruised and bloodied from some madman that had used you hard?"

From the man who had tied her up and beat her until her skin had flayed, all because she had had no one to protect her. After her father's death when she was ten and her mother's death when she was fourteen, she had been completely on her own. And, fool that she had been, she had thought she had been in control of her life in a way that only a sixteen-year-old girl selling herself to pay for her train tickets out west could. Until she had barely survived a fate that so many whores didn't.

And it had been Mistress who had rescued her. A dove at the hotel had contacted Mistress to say that there was a girl—a child, really—who had been beaten while whoring. Mistress had paid the doctor and taken Emmy home, nursing her back to health. Teaching her manners and social graces, teaching her how to whore properly, with as little risk and harm done as possible. How to be more than just a common harlot with a pretty head of hair and luxurious tits, as Hank would say.

Mistress had made her Emerald Green, the second most famous whore this side of the Mississippi. Maybe in the whole of the country.

And Emmy knew she was being ungrateful to walk away from that.

But then again, Mistress was counting on that feeling of obligation. That was how she kept girls in her thrall, kept them from marrying their patrons. Not all of them—some walked away just like this, still others slipped off into the night, spirited away by Free Cyrus Franklin, maybe.

"I couldn't forget that if I tried," Emmy said,

sitting back and keeping her voice level. "And God knows, I've tried. But what of you? It hasn't been a month since you were willing to let me go to a man who would tie me up again, all because Raymond was late. I haven't forgotten. Have you?"

The flash of shame on Mistress's face was gone so quickly that Emmy wasn't sure it'd been there at all. Instead, righteous indignation bloomed in shame's place. "I wouldn't have let him hurt you!"

"Nor will he ever have the chance. I thank you for everything you've done and I will do my part to make sure that Raymond continues to treat the Jeweled Ladies with the respect you and the girls deserve."

Mistress notched an eyebrow at her. Was it possible the woman hadn't considered that a former Jewel having the mayor's ear was a point in her favor? "And what of Mr. O'Shea?"

Emmy rolled her eyes. "What of him? He's Raymond's man of business."

Mistress tilted her head back and forth. "No," she said calmly, "I don't think he is. He knows too much. Far, *far* too much."

Like what it was to work on his back—or knees. Like who Emmy had been—and who Emily had been.

"I do not like Mr. O'Shea," Emmy said, ignoring the way her pulse quickened just talking about him. "But I see how Raymond uses him. Raymond is above the fray and mudslinging of politics—"

"But not above marrying a whore," Mistress said under her breath.

Emmy ignored her. "Mr. O'Shea is the muscle Raymond needs to keep his hands clean. He serves a purpose for Raymond's career. He is invaluable for

119

Raymond's rise in power and for that, I must tolerate him."

Although 'tolerate him' was not precisely how Emmy would describe their time in bed together where Hank's hands had stayed very, very dirty. Hank had made her come apart—easily. God, that feeling—she could get addicted to it as some got addicted to laudanum. She did not like him, necessarily, but she was placing a great deal of faith in him.

Mistress heaved a mighty sigh. "You're risking everything, you know that."

Nothing risked, nothing gained. "I'm leaving, Emily, with or without your blessing."

Mistress rubbed her temples. "When?"

"Today." Yes, she loved Raymond and yes, Hank could make her shatter, seemingly on command and, yes, between them, she would have security and protection and maybe even a family. She could have everything.

But most of all, she wouldn't have to pretend. The greatest actress of her age could slip off quietly into the sunset and none would be the wiser.

An honest life beckoned to her from the other side. Well, she'd still be pretending in public. But she could be honest for more than just a few hours every Tuesday night with Raymond. Her legs would only spread for the pleasure of two men and that, considering how very many men she'd spread for, was something for which to be thankful for, indeed.

Mistress made a noise of disgust as she threw her hands up. It was the most unladylike Emmy had ever seen her. "Just like that? Do you have any idea what a disruption that will cause?"

Emmy shrugged. "Find a new gem." She stood and smoothed out her skirts. "It's high time you had a Diamond, no matter how rough, Mistress."

Mistress scowled, but Emmy went on. "I shall require a new wardrobe befitting of Raymond's wife. I was hoping to use Ebony's services. The local seamstresses cannot compete with her skills, if that's all right with you." And, in all honesty, she had a feeling that she was going to need a friend in the coming months of what otherwise would be near-total social isolation. There was no good way to justify seeing Sapphire, but Ebony would be able to come to Mrs. Logan's for long afternoons of fittings and tea and it would be a relief.

"Will you pay for her time?"

Emmy smiled, a real smile this time. This was the right choice. "But of course." She turned to go.

"Emmeline?"

She stilled at that name—her true name. She'd better get used to hearing it again, though, since Emerald Green was in her death throes and Emmeline was about to emerge from the ashes. "Yes?"

Mistress stood and came around her desk. She put her hands on Emmy's shoulders and stared into her eyes. "You, more than any other girl here, have been the daughter of my heart." And before Emmy could process *that* thought, Mistress had crushed her into a firm hug. "My door is always open to you," she whispered into Emmy's ear. "If you need me…"

Unexpected tears pooled in Emmy's eyes as she returned the embrace. It wasn't like Mistress to be sentimental, but then, nothing stayed the same forever, did it? "Thank you, Emily."

Then, as quickly as the emotion had appeared, it was gone. Mistress released her and all but marched back to her desk. "I won't be at the wedding. I'm sure you prefer it that way."

She wouldn't be there to watch Emmy be reborn as a proper woman with a respectable future ahead of her. And no one would see Mistress's wet eyes.

"Thank you, Mistress," Emmy whispered. With that, she took her leave.

And was Emerald Green no more.

Chapter Eleven

Are you all right, darling?" Raymond asked as he sat on the settee with Emmy in Mrs. Logan's sitting room. "You seem pensive."

"I'm not pensive," she said with a sigh. "I'm *bored*. How do women sit around knitting all day?"

"It's an acquired skill, dearie," Mrs. Logan interjected from her seat near the window, where she was actively knitting. "You'll get used to it."

Emmy sighed again and rested her head on Raymond's shoulder. It wasn't quite as good as curling up in bed next to her, but it was close. "Only another two months until we're married," he reminded her, stroking her shoulder.

"An eternity," Emmy whispered. "I'm so lonely, Raymond. I never thought I'd miss being Emerald Green but..."

"But you've had no one in your bed for a month and you miss it?" He kept his voice pitched low, so Mrs. Logan wouldn't hear. Not that Mrs. Logan could hear much of anything, anyway. Nor did she object to Raymond and Emmy curling up like this—as long as their clothes stayed on, she figured that was good enough. Still, Raymond didn't want the older woman to hear his and Emmy's private talks.

She nodded. "I miss you. I think I even miss Hank, just a little."

He chuckled at that and pressed a kiss to her forehead that, to him at least, felt chaste. But he put as much heat as he could into it. Mrs. Logan was watching, after all, and Raymond had to get better at meaning Emmy had *luscious tits* with every word he said and move he made.

Not that it was easy right now. Her new dresses were—well, perhaps not 'modest,' not by comparison to some of the most respectable ladies in town. But instead of revealing her bosom, the neckline of the dresses came almost up to her collarbones. And the sleeves—she wore actual sleeves now. True, they came only to her elbows, but she now always wore gloves in public and paired the whole look with a fine shawl and a bonnet. In general, she was quite covered from head to toe.

But the dresses still clung to her figure— Raymond caught himself—her luscious tits. When he escorted her to the Golden Star Hotel for a lunch, men still looked at her as if they might like to open a tab. For the first time in his life, Raymond was finding himself in the grip of jealousy. Which, Hank had assured him, was a good thing. Apparently, being jealous of his gorgeous wife-to-be went hand-in-hand with an appreciation of her body.

"He misses you too, darling," Raymond cooed in her ear. And it was true. Lying in his arms at night—on the few nights Hank had managed to sneak into the house unnoticed—he'd confided that he looked forward to the time when it would be the three of them in bed.

"You're all hard and muscled," Hank had explained

124

when Raymond had questioned him. "And she's all... soft. Her softness makes you all the harder," he'd added, gripping Raymond's rod and bringing it back to life with a few firm pulls. And then they'd tumbled into each other's arms again and...

"You're thinking of him right now, aren't you?" Emmy scolded in the barest whisper. "Not fair. At least tell me you two aren't sucking off at the office. You promised."

"We're not. Mostly," he added, just to rile her up.

She swatted at him with a laugh and he playfully caught her wrist in his hand. Behind them, Mrs. Logan cleared her throat. "Tea, Mayor Dupree?" she asked, shuffling past them to her small kitchen without waiting for an answer.

"Bless her heart," Raymond said when the older woman was gone. Every night Raymond came to visit, Mrs. Logan would sit nearby—until she came up with a convenient excuse to be gone from the room for ten or fifteen minutes at a time.

"So, tell me how it's going with Hank," Emmy said, keeping her voice quiet.

"He sent you a note." This was a game they'd started playing, a way for Emmy and Hank to court, in their own way. They sent short letters to each other through Raymond—scandalous notes, to be sure.

Raymond didn't understand half of what made Emmy blush at the thought of the notes—or Hank laugh with glee when he read Emmy's sharp responses. But the two of them were clearly enjoying the flirting, so who was Raymond to question it?

He slipped the note out of his jacket pocket and watched as Emmy tucked it into the bodice of her modest gown. "That's wonderful, darling—but tell me about *you* and Hank," she insisted.

Raymond sighed, curling his arms around her even more. He nuzzled his face into the crook of her neck and breathed in Emmy's sweet smell. "It's… God, darling, it's everything I ever wanted."

She laced her fingers through his hair. If Mrs. Logan walked back into the room at this exact moment, he and Emmy would look very much like they were in a lover's embrace. "Almost everything," Raymond corrected. "He moves in in two weeks. He had to find someone to take his place at the boarding house—and offer Mrs. Bund more money so she would publically ask him to leave."

Raymond had a head for politics, but Hank operated at a deeper level than Raymond ever would. Raymond would have just had Hank quit the boarding house and relocate to his house. But Hank had insisted a public break with Mrs. Bund—over the price of room and board—was required to allay any suspicion.

Until then, Hank would 'work late'—at Raymond's house—on the nights when the servants weren't required.

"Last night," Raymond went on, unwilling to waste a moment of his time with Emmy, "he…" His cheeks heated. It wasn't that he was ashamed of what he and Hank did—Emmy certainly never made him feel that way.

But admitting how Hank had touched him in Mrs. Logan's parlor was not the most comfortable of experiences.

"Go on," Emmy whispered into his hair. "Someone should be getting satisfaction, even if it's not me."

"He said he is training my body to take him in." Just thinking about it made him hard in his trousers again. "He slipped two fingers into my body."

Which was not an adequate way to describe what Hank had done to him. He'd bent Raymond over the footboard of the bed and applied a balm of some kind—cool and smooth—to his asshole. While Hank stroked Raymond's rod in an unhurried fashion, he'd kissed and nibbled at the bare muscles of Raymond's back and shoulders and neck, and while he was doing all of that—he really was quite skilled—he'd been massaging the lotion into Raymond's body. His finger—just the tip—would press up until Raymond's body gave and accepted him.

And Raymond—his cheeks burning, his rod straining—he knew that he should be ashamed of the wave of pleasure that had washed over him. He should be ashamed of letting Hank bend him over and spread his legs and his cheeks and, most of all, he should be horrified that he allowed that touch.

That he encouraged it.

That he wanted it more.

Because he had. As Hank had slowly worked first one finger into Raymond's body and then, when he'd decided Raymond was ready for it, a second finger, Raymond had bucked and writhed and begged for more. Begged for the release that only Hank could give him.

And through it all, Hank had stood behind him, his glorious rod rubbing against Raymond's hip and ass, and he had whispered the most sinful things to Raymond. How good it felt to feel his body closing around Hank's fingers. How much he wanted to slide his cock into

127

Raymond and fuck him *so* hard. How, next time, they'd switch positions and Raymond could do this to him—could finger him, could fuck him, could tie him to the bedpost and come all over his chest, if he wanted. How Raymond could make Hank his in every single way. And soon, Emmy would join them, her soft mounds of flesh pressed against their hardness, her wantonness a perfect match for their wickedness.

He clutched Emmy even tighter as the memory washed over him. He still didn't want to lie with her the way Hank had—but there was no denying the power of the images Hank described for him. And Raymond knew, with ever-growing certainty, that he could never even dream of another woman naked in bed with him and Hank.

Emmy kissed his forehead as she processed this information. "How did it feel?"

Raymond's heart squeezed with love for this woman, for there wasn't a bit of judgment in her voice, nor an iota of disgust. "It was... it was odd. Wonderfully so—I felt so..."

"So full?"

"Yes!" She understood. Well, of course she would. If anyone could understand the strange sensation of opening your body up to another and giving them permission to join with you, it would be his Emmy. "Yes, that's it exactly. He was moving inside of me and he had a grip on my rod and it was..." he shuddered, fighting down the rising erection.

"It didn't..." she swallowed nervously. "It didn't hurt?"

"No." He leaned back to look at Emmy. "Really, darling, it was fine. Better than fine. He prepared me."

"Oh." She dropped her gaze, her cheeks a bright red. "I just... I am glad it didn't hurt."

He thought about her reaction—it was unlike Emmy to not wholeheartedly embrace bed play. And then he remembered—when they'd first set the rules, Emmy had said that no one could play with her other hole.

"Did it hurt for you, then?" he asked gently.

She shrugged. "Some men like that sort of thing—with women, too," she quickly added. "But I guess the balm and going slow—it must make a difference."

Raymond pulled her into a firm hug because he understood what she wasn't saying. Whoever had done to her what Hank was going to do to him hadn't had creams and patience.

He could just imagine the pain if Hank had taken his thick rod and shoved it directly into Raymond's body. He shuddered to think of it. "It's not like that at all," he promised her. "It was wonderful, the slide of his body in mine."

She was silent for a moment longer. "Did you scream in pleasure?" Her breath had caught and instinctively, Raymond slid his hand down her body, down her thigh. "He promised you would and I expect you to hold him to that, Raymond." She shifted against him, soft against his hard. "I've held you for so long and so only once have I been part of your satisfaction. I want to see you *shatter*."

"You do? You really don't mind?"

She shook her head. "To see him bring you such happiness? Of course not. Not any more than you minded watching him fuck me."

"Emmy!" Raymond's cheeks grew hot again. She wasn't supposed to speak like that anymore. At least, not outside of the bedroom and they had several more months to go before they got back to that room together. "My dear!"

But she just laughed and, at that moment, Mrs. Logan appeared with a tea tray balanced in her hands. She *harrumphed* loudly as Raymond and Emmy disentangled themselves and resumed a more proper posture on the settee together.

"I do wish we could move the date of the wedding up," Emmy said in a voice meant to carry to Mrs. Logan.

The rest of the evening passed uneventfully. Raymond kept up a polite stream of conversation fit for mixed company. The schoolmarm, Miss Krenshaw, had welcomed the addition of new readers and slates for the children that Emmy had purchased, but Raymond wasn't sure Emmy had won the upright woman over.

Reverend Mays, however, was positively ecstatic at the addition of new stained glass windows to the Methodist church. His church would have the first stained glass in Brimstone—"a sure sign of God's blessing!" he had crowed in Raymond's office. What's more, Raymond had secured the promise from Rev. Mays that he would not only publically thank Emmeline McCartney for the windows, but he would welcome her with open arms to the fold.

Which, Emmy had laughed, had nothing to do with the fact that the good Reverend had been a regular patron at the Jeweled Ladies for years.

Eventually, their time together came to an end. "Thursday for lunch, my darling?" Raymond said.

Mrs. Logan *harrumphed* again, which Raymond took as a good sign that his ability to say one thing and mean another about Emmy's tits was getting better. Emmy smiled her approval and then Mrs. Logan disappeared so they could say their good-byes in the narrow entry hall of her house.

"I didn't scream," Raymond said when he had Emmy wrapped in an almost passionate embrace. Because he realized that he'd never answered her question. "I shattered, as you put it, darling—but I didn't scream."

She touched his face lovingly. "You will. In his hands, you will have no choice. God, I cannot wait to see it."

He grinned down at her. "So wicked, my darling."

"For you," she said in all seriousness. "All for you, Raymond."

He clutched her to his chest and murmured his love for her into her hair before they touched lips together, just in case Mrs. Logan was peeking. This, at least, was getting easier. Before Hank, Raymond had kissed very few people. Practice—with either man or woman—made for a reasonable facsimile of perfection.

Mrs. Logan reappeared as they broke apart and opened the door for Raymond. Raymond settled his hat on his head, and with a final look back at Emmy, headed down into the street.

It was dark, the dusk light fading into a brilliant purple sky. Raymond strolled along, humming to himself as he appreciated the night sky, the beautiful woman he had just left and the beautiful man waiting for him. Eventually. Hank would slip into the house

131

after he'd put in his public appearance in a saloon and then slip out again in the morning before the sun rose. But for a few glorious hours, he and Raymond would be free to explore each other.

A dark shape moved at the edge of his vision and Raymond slowed. Streetlamps—that's what this town needed. Gas lanterns lighting the streets after dark would reduce crime and fear.

The shape moved toward Raymond and he stopped. He had his walking stick with him—he always took it when he was out after dark.

"Ah, our illustrious mayor," a deep voice rumbled.

Raymond internally winced. He knew that voice—that shape. Judge Gerard Hobson was on the prowl. "Your honor," Raymond said, resuming a leisurely walk. "What brings you out on this fine evening?"

"A walk clears the mind," Hobson replied as if they were having a regular conversation.

But Raymond knew that wasn't possible. Hobson hated Raymond, hated the fact that Raymond had succeeded his father Leopold for the mayor's office—handily beating Hobson in the election. And the reelection.

As judge, Hobson wielded a great deal of power in Brimstone. But not as much as Raymond did.

If only Raymond had Hank with him. But as soon as that thought crossed his mind, Raymond pushed it away. He didn't want Hobson to think there was anything more than a working relationship between them.

"Oh? And what clarity has this lovely evening brought to you?" Raymond asked, picking up the pace ever-so-slightly.

Hobson matched him effortlessly. It really was a crying shame the man was such a heartless bastard

132

because there was a certain appeal to his silver hair, his smooth mustache, even his penchant for dressing in black and silver.

He was handsome. Except for his eyes. They showed Hobson for what he really was—tight and hard and unbending. For years now, Hobson had worked to undermine the Duprees. Raymond's father had always brushed the judge's actions off—but whatever their feud had been, it hadn't died with Leopold and Isabelle Dupree. Would that it had because Raymond didn't particularly enjoy being in direct opposition to the judge.

But he was.

"I was just thinking how pleased I am that you shall be marrying that… woman," Hobson said, unable to get the last word out without grimacing. "Indeed, I cannot imagine a finer match." He stopped and extended a hand to Raymond. "Congratulations. I'm sure your parents would be proud of you."

Raymond eyed the outstretched hand with suspicion because Hobson had never cared for Raymond's parents. He hadn't even attended their funerals, for God's sake. "Really, Hobson. What's this about?"

Hobson shrugged. If he were offended that Raymond hadn't shaken his hand, he didn't show it. "You're marrying the most notorious woman in Texas. It makes my life so much easier." He chuckled as Raymond began to walk away from him. "Enjoy your whore, Raymond. She's going to cost you your career."

Before Raymond could even respond, Hobson was off, whistling a happy tune as he disappeared back into the shadows.

Raymond stood there for a long moment. Hobson was wrong and that was all there was to it. Emmy wasn't going to bring him down—he was going to lift her up. He and Hank and Emmy had gone over this. He was doing the Christian thing, bringing Emmy out of sin and into the eyes of the Church as a proper, married woman. He'd been devoted for months. It was obviously a love match and besides, outside of Brimstone, few would care that Emmy used to be a whore.

Because she wasn't. Emerald Green no longer existed and Emmeline McCartney would soon be Mrs. Emmeline Dupree—and the Dupree name was above reproach.

Raymond shook his doubts out of his head. Hobson was blowing smoke, that was all. Yes, the older man would continue to be a problem, but Raymond—and Hank—had handled the man before and they would handle him again.

But it just reinforced that there was no room to make a mistake here. He and Emmy had to be wildly, perfectly in love. Hank had to be nothing more than a man of business. And Raymond...

Raymond wouldn't make a mistake. He *couldn't*.

Chapter Twelve

Hank did not like Tuesdays. Raymond went courting Emmy and Hank was charged with being out in public. He'd found he liked playing cards at the Golden Star hotel best. The doves there weren't too pushy and the whiskey wasn't too watered down. The music wasn't half bad, either. It was the sort of place a man could tolerate.

But still, he couldn't fight the nervous energy that gripped him from the moment he walked into the joint. A month into this experiment had left him craving the comforts of home.

Him! Of all people, he wanted to be at home with Raymond. Hell, he even missed Emmy because, aside from that one glorious night, he hadn't had her again. He hadn't even seen her, outside of stopping by Mrs. Logan's home to make sure that Emmy had, in fact, gotten settled into the old widow's house. All he had was an occasional note where she tried to cut him to shreds with sexual innuendo. She was winning, too. He ached to bury himself in her.

Mrs. Logan, it turned out, had done some time on her back before she'd met Mr. Logan decades ago. And even if she hadn't been willing to lend the sheen of respectability to Emmy on her own, money talked and Mrs. Logan needed the cash. Mr. Logan had not been a wealthy man when he'd passed.

Not that the old woman had admitted to any of that, nor had Hank thought to mention what he knew. But Hank had looked long and hard before settling on the woman and who better to help rehabilitate a soiled dove than one of her kind?

"Two cards," he said, trying to focus on his game. He won some, he lost more—losing wasn't his favorite. He'd worked too hard for his money over the years to willingly piss it away. But there was value in letting people think he wasn't all that bright.

He got his cards—nothing. So he folded and watched as Kerr, the undertaker, tried to match wits with a professional gambler. Kerr, Hank decided, was going to lose everything in about five seconds.

Which he did. As Hank watched the drama play out—Kerr accused the gambler of cheating and the gambler egged Kerr on—the back of his neck prickled with the familiar feeling of someone watching him.

Hank drained his whiskey and turned to yell for more—and found himself squarely in the sights of none other than Judge Gerard Hobson.

Well. It'd taken the man long enough to make his move. Now all Hank had to do was see how it'd play out.

Kerr was shouting now—the whole reason Raymond had banned guns in this town in one argument—so Hank excused himself from the table and moved toward the bar. Unsurprisingly, Hobson was by his side in moments. "O'Shea," he said gruffly.

"Your honor," Hank said calmly as he ordered his whiskey.

Hobson ordered the same, but he didn't say anything. Which wasn't like the man. Gerard Hobson never had any trouble passing judgment on anyone in this town. He was the law, regardless of the sheriff, and he enforced it with an iron fist.

In his fifties with silver hair and impeccable clothes—all black, of course, except for the starched white linen shirt—and a silver pin set into the black tie he wore around his neck, the man might have been handsome, if he hadn't cultivated such a mean look about him.

He was a hard man, Hobson was. As best Hank could tell, both from his own digging and what Raymond had told him, Hobson had been Leopold Dupree's protégée until the two men had had a falling out some thirty years ago. There was no record of what had created the rift, but Hank had a theory—and that theory had everything to do with Isabelle Dupree. Who had married Leopold and borne him a son.

Raymond.

Since then, there'd been no love lost between the families. It didn't matter that Leopold and Isabelle Dupree were dead. Hobson operated under the assumption that Brimstone was his by rights and the fact that a Dupree sat in the mayor's office instead of a Hobson was something the man couldn't let stand.

But the hell of it was, aside from the long-standing feud with the Dupree family, there was nothing on Hobson. No visits to whorehouses or even the Jeweled Ladies. No vices aside from cigars and whiskey, no gaming, no peccadillos—nothing. *Nothing* Hank could use for leverage. Hobson was as pure as the driven snow. Not that it snowed much in this part of Texas.

Hank knew he had to be careful because, as hard and ruthless as Hobson was, he was no idiot. He was something else entirely.

He was dangerous. By all appearances, he was without sin and he had a huge bag of stones ready to throw.

But even for all that, he was not unpredictable. Hank had reasoned this might happen, what with Raymond and Emmy announcing their engagement and Emmy leaving the Jeweled Ladies behind. Hobson smelled blood on the water, no doubt, and if he had his way, he'd churn until they all drowned.

"So you're still working for our illustrious mayor," Hobson finally began, when Hank was almost done with his whiskey. Behind them, Kerr the undertaker was being forcibly removed from the saloon.

"Aye," Hank said evenly. "And you're still running the court." Because they could stand around stating the obvious all night long.

"He's going to marry that whore," Hobson said, spitting out the last word as if it'd left a vile taste in his mouth.

Icy calm burned away the fire of the whiskey in his belly. He knew this feeling—the way his body readied for a fight. But Hank pushed back against it. If he took out the judge over a slight to Emmy, the gossip would be merciless. And he was not going to let Hobson goad him into anything so stupid as a fistfight in the Golden Star hotel. "He's smitten, he is," Hank went on, trying to color his tone with a bit of disbelief. He wasn't sure he made it.

He turned to face Hobson and was surprised to see the man was... smiling? "Just like his father,"

Hobson said, swallowing his whiskey in one long gulp and waving for the bartender. "Duprees never could stay away from a pretty harlot."

Hank said nothing except to shrug as if the past didn't interest him. But he'd been right—Hobson had wanted Raymond's mother and had lost her to Leopold.

"You," Hobson went on, slapping Hank on the shoulder as if they were the very best of friends, "should come work for me, O'Shea. Our illustrious mayor is shooting himself in the foot over a trollop. His career won't survive this and I could have a... use for you."

Once, when he'd been about twelve, Hank had lived in an alley behind a firehouse in Boston. The little space he'd created had been sheltered from the worst of the wind and the snow and the firefighters had taken pity on the urchin he'd been and left food out for him. He'd even played with the spotted dog they'd kept. It'd been almost decent, until the firehouse itself had burned to the ground.

But every time an alarm went up, a huge, clanging bell would be rung—all the louder because it was located just on the other side of the wall where Hank slept. That bell had never rung for anything good.

Hank heard that bell now, ringing loud and clear in his ears. Because all his old instincts about what a man said when he was looking for a boy came rushing back.

I could have a use for you.

It was possible, Hank tried to reason as the bartender poured Hobson another shot of whiskey, that Hobson wasn't aware of the other meaning his words carried. But then again, it was possible those words were entirely intentional. And if they were—how much did Hobson know? Or was he just firing a shot into the dark, hoping to get lucky? "Aye? Like what?"

Hobson ran his gaze over Hank's shoulders, his arms. The bell clanging in Hank's head only got louder, but he was not going to show this man anything. Instead, he notched an eyebrow and tried to look bored. And stupid. It was a struggle.

"Dupree's too prissy to get his hands dirty," Hobson said, turning back to his whiskey. Hank fought a sigh of relief. "That's why he has you."

"Aye," Hank agreed because that, at least, was common knowledge. He operated at the very farthest edge of the law, when he had to. All to protect Raymond.

Everything to protect Raymond.

He had to keep his poker face up because there was so much more at stake now. This wasn't just a political career. This was their life together. This was his chance at a fairy-tale ending, where he got the king *and* the princess and they all lived happily ever after.

All he had to do was slay a few dragons—and Hobson was the biggest dragon in the land right now.

Hobson glanced at Hank out of the corner of his eye. "How much does he pay you?"

"Enough," Hank said simply.

"Enough to lose, anyway," Hobson agreed, sounding far too pleased with himself. "I can offer you more."

I doubt it. But Hank kept the words off his tongue. Instead, he said, "How do you mean?" in as dumb a voice as he could manage.

Something in Hobson's gaze sharpened and Hank knew he'd overplayed his hand. The judge leaned closer to Hank and the air felt sharp. Hank immediately regretted not strapping his knife to his back. Guns may be illegal inside city limits, but a man liked to be prepared.

And Hank was not prepared for Hobson.

"You're an intelligent man, O'Shea," Hobson said in a voice that was almost mesmerizing for the power it carried. "It does not behoove you to play dumb with me."

Hank recognized that power and what it meant. So it hadn't been an accidental turn of phrase, then. Hobson would use him and, what's more, Hobson would enjoy it. Every single bit of it.

His mind flashed back to, of all things, carrying Emmy up the stairs in Raymond's house little more than a month ago. To her saying that she would not be tied and beaten, to feeling the tremor of fear that had coursed through her otherwise naked and aroused body.

A whore was paid to like what her patrons liked. Hank knew it as well as anyone.

But very few knew what he knew about Emmy. About how she'd been tied and horsewhipped and then left for dead. How Emily Witherspoon—Mistress— had come to her rescue and turned her into the finest lady of the night.

Had it been Hobson? Because Hank knew—*knew*, deep in his gut—that the man was capable of it. That he preyed on the fear and the pain.

And that was how he wanted Hank. Afraid. The fear was more arousing than the pain and Hobson wanted it *all*.

141

A lesser man might give it to him. But Hank had a lifetime of holding onto himself, of keeping his mind and his body separate while he did what he had to in order to survive.

And he was not about to give Hobson the satisfaction.

"Aye," he agreed, smiling as affably as he could. "Just like it doesn't behoove you to sink to my level, now does it?" He pointedly looked at Hobson's hands.

Hobson's lips twisted then into something that was not now nor ever would be a smile. "My boy," he said, his voice a silky whisper studded with nails, "you have no idea, do you?"

My boy.

The false endearment clanged around his head louder than any bell ever would. For so many years, he'd been nothing but a boy to men like this—men of quality, men who enforced morals for other people, who wrote the laws and condemned the sinners and then turned around and bought twenty minutes of time in a boy's mouth or his arse because they simply *could*. And they would grab onto his ears like they were handles on a pitcher and jerk his head around until his ears felt permanently maimed and he choked on their spunk because that's what they paid him for—to do whatever they wanted with him.

Because who would stop them?

No one, that's who. Except for now. Hank was no one's boy. Not anymore. He was Raymond's, heart and soul, but he would never again be someone's nameless, faceless *boy*. It was time to put an end to the pleasantries.

Hobson went on, "Think of what I could offer you. Power. Wealth. He pays you enough? I can give you more. Five thousand, to start. And after you prove your worth..." his gaze traveled Hank's chest. "There's no limit to what you could earn, working for me."

Hell. Five thousand was a lot of money—more than enough to start over somewhere as a man of consequence. And maybe a year ago, Hank would have taken that chance.

He would have thought of himself—and no one else.

But now? Now Raymond was more to him than a means to an end. And Hank could not be bought.

Not that Hobson knew that. Hank leaned in close to the judge, closer than he wanted to be. He inhaled deeply, memorizing the combination of bay rum and pipe tobacco and... and books. The man had a tinge of paper to his scent.

There wasn't a single note of femininity to him. No note of lilac or vanilla, of lavender or even lemons that drifted on his shoulders from a lover's touch in the morning. Just bay rum, tobacco and paper. Hank wouldn't forget it.

Hobson's eyes grew wider, but it was his only reaction to Hank. "Listen and listen good, Hobson," he said under his breath, his words meant for one set of ears only. "Stay clear of them."

"Or?" he replied easily, his eyes darkening with the challenge and Hank knew that Hobson would be happy to meet that challenge. But Hank said nothing. "Or what, Mr. O'Shea? Are you making threats against the law?" He shook his head in mock disappointment. "And for what? For Dupree? He's going to burn in hell for his sins."

Hank leaned back. He would not explain himself

143

and he would not repeat himself. To do so would be an insult to both of their intelligences. Instead he took a long sip of his whiskey.

Very likely, Hobson knew exactly what Hank was capable of. Just because Hank had never been named as the criminal in question didn't mean that people didn't talk. And just as likely, those skills were what Hobson wanted.

"Or maybe I've read this wrong," Hobson went on, sounding amused. "Maybe you're doing it for *her*. Maybe," he went on with a chuckle, "that whore's got you both by the balls."

"Is that what you think of, all alone at night, your hands wrapped around your little sausage of a prick?" Hank *tsked*. "Didn't figure that for your style, Hobson. Men go to hell for far less."

Hobson's humor, both real and forced, fell away and Hank had to fight the shiver that raced down his back. "Did you know," he said in a carefully controlled voice, "that Hank O'Shea didn't exist before three years ago?"

"You searched all of bonnie Ireland, did you?" Hank replied, letting his accent come in strong waves. He wasn't surprised that Hobson had dug into him. The man was no idiot. No sense in wasting a perfectly good opportunity to misdirect the man. Because he'd never find Hank O'Shea in any parish register back in Ireland.

"I'll find the truth—before this election," Hobson promised. He finished his whiskey. "And when I do," he added, setting his glass back on the bar with a *thunk*, "Dupree will be out and you and I will discuss what employment options remain open to a man of your particular… skills." He stood. "Brimstone will be a moral town, Mr. O'Shea. I will *make* it so."

His first thoughts were of Raymond and Emmy, of the life they were going to keep behind closed doors. But Mistress and the others at the Jeweled Ladies—they crossed his mind, too. They were all in danger. "And here I thought only the Lord could take his vengeance."

Hobson smiled wide, the lamplight gleaming off his white teeth. "A man like you knows the truth, Mr. O'Shea."

"Aye? And what truth is that?"

"That sometimes, the Angel of Death is welcomed far more than the Angel of Mercy." He set his fine beaver hat on his head and tipped it toward Hank. "My regards to your boss. And his *whore*."

Hank watched the man walk away. His gut told him to get up, go find Raymond and Emmy and guard them with his life because they *were* his life.

But he didn't. He didn't even head over to the Jeweled Ladies. Instead, he ordered another round of whiskey and took his place back at the gaming table where, in short order, he took the gambler for everything he was worth—and everything Kerr had been worth.

He was done playing around.

Chapter Thirteen

Raymond couldn't help it. He started to shake in Hank's arms after Hank had told him about his confrontation with Judge Hobson.

"Hank," Raymond said, his voice shaking, "why is he doing this?"

Hank sighed. "I think it's about a woman. And I'm sorry to say, I think it's about your mother."

"But she's dead! She's been dead for years now!"

Hank chuckled, although there was no joy in it. "You don't understand him," he said, wrapping his arms around Raymond's shoulders. "But I do. He's a hard man, obsessive and focused and he doesn't like losing. He values control more than anything else. If I had to guess, I would say your mother took that away from him. And he's been trying to get it back ever since."

"But what does that have to do with me?" Raymond hated how pitiful he sounded because he did not fancy himself to be a pitiful man. But Hank was right—Raymond did not understand Hobson.

"Every time he sees you, he sees his failure. It's really that simple." Hank kissed Raymond's forehead. "You let me handle this."

Oh, that was a tempting offer because, after all,

that was what Hank did. But Hobson wasn't some criminal coming through town on his way to Mexico or some cattle baron who was too full of himself. He had the full weight of the law behind him and everyone knew it. "What happens if he wins?"

Hank sighed, as if the possibility wasn't even worth discussing. "He might," he conceded. "But he wouldn't be reelected. People may say they want a moral town, but there are four brothels in this town and they all keep up a steady stream of business. People don't want to live as they're supposed to. If Hobson wins the mayor's office, he'll shut down the brothels and maybe even the saloons. He'll tighten his grip on this town until no one can breathe and people won't like it. They'll learn their mistake soon enough and then he'll be out. Besides," he went on, pulling the sheet up over Raymond's chest, "you're going to keep moving forward. Austin is a different town. They'll get this constitution settled and you'll be elected to the statehouse and Hobson won't be a problem anymore."

He sounded confident—maybe too confident. But then, Hank had never led him wrong before. "But what if he finds out about us? What if he finds out about you?" More than the risk to his career, that terrified Raymond. People lost elections all the time. It was an unpleasant reality, but an acceptable one. However, if people knew what he did with Hank—and what they would both do with Emmy—there would be no coming back from that. All three of their reputations would be permanently blackened.

Hank was silent for a long time, his hands skimming up and down over Raymond's shoulders and arms. "Then we leave. We start over someplace else.

147

San Francisco, maybe. Somewhere where no one has ever heard of Brimstone or Emerald Green." And, although he didn't say it, Raymond heard it anyway—where no one had ever heard of the Duprees.

"But we could all be arrested—*jailed.*"

Hank leaned back and tilted Raymond's face up to look him in the eyes. "Aye, I knew that was a risk when we started. But you're worth the risk."

Raymond kissed him then—a kiss of promise and of hope and, yes, of a little bit of fear. He was terrified that he would lose this—this happiness, this peace, and this pleasure—but Hank was right. Raymond had known the risks when they'd started and even knowing what he knew now about Hobson, he would've taken the same risk all over again.

"I'll take care of it," Hank whispered as they rolled into each other, hands and mouths and rods everywhere. "I will take care of you, my beautiful man."

*

"I didn't expect to see you back here," Mistress said as Hank settled into what he was beginning to think of as his chair in the Jeweled Ladies' parlor. "Are you here for personal reasons?" Mistress batted her eyes at him. "I'll admit that I had been hoping to see you again."

Hank snorted. "Is there somewhere we could talk in private?"

"My bedroom," she suggested with a purr in her voice.

"I was thinking more along the lines of an office,"

148

Hank replied. "Although you do tempt me, Mistress," he offered as a concession.

She pouted, but he could tell it wasn't anything more than playacting. "Not enough, apparently." So gracefully that she practically floated, Mistress rose to her feet and beckoned for him to follow. "This way."

Hank followed her upstairs to a sparse room located directly above the parlor. This was clearly her private domain, the office of the brothel. He wondered how many men had ever seen the inside of this room before.

"Have a seat," she said in a voice that was utterly devoid of purring or cooing of any kind.

He grinned as he did what he was told. Finally, he was talking with the real Mistress. "I have a problem that may be of interest to you," he began with no other introduction.

Mistress narrowed her eyes as she sat in the chair behind the desk. "Does this problem involve a bed and the removal of all of our clothing? Or even some of it?"

"No, Mistress."

She scowled—which was not a big movement. It was more the twisting of the lips to one side, but Hank saw it for what it was. "The only other place I can think of our interests intersecting would be one of my girls marrying your boss. And as Miss Green no longer works at the Jeweled Ladies and is therefore no longer one of my girls, it's hard to see where our interests overlap at all."

In other words, her patience with him was wearing thin.

"Would you turn your back on Emmy in her time of need?"

149

"Don't toy with me, Mr. O'Shea," she snapped—which only made Hank grin all the more. He was seeing the real woman in her natural environment—and it was a rare and wondrous thing. Mistress was not to be taken lightly. "Of course I wouldn't turn my back on Emmy. She was like a daughter to me."

He cut to the chase. "What do you know about Judge Hobson?"

The effect of those words—that name—was immediate. The color drained out of her face and she became very still. "*Is* there a problem?"

She was scared. Then again, she had a good right to be. "Not yet. But I don't think it will stay that way for long and I can't find anything on the man. Not a damned thing."

Mistress dropped her gaze to the surface of her desk for a moment as she put her thoughts in order. Hank gave her the time. Because he knew what she was thinking—Hank had managed to uncover the name Emily Witherspoon. It was perhaps one of Mistress's most closely guarded secrets—and he had ferreted it out. But he couldn't find a single thing to hold over Hobson. And if he wanted to keep Raymond and Emmy safe, he had to come up with something—fast.

"Judge Hobson is a fine, upstanding member of the Brimstone community," Mistress said in a tone that was more forced than genial.

"He's also a threat to both of us," Hank said quietly. "It's bad enough that he wants to ruin Dupree—but he wants to be mayor, too. He'll shut you down, Mistress. He'll go for the other whorehouses first, but he *will* come for you. You know it and I know it. He doesn't just want to run this town, he wants control. He wants to make every single person in this town beg." Mistress got paler as Hank spoke. "He's the kind of man who won't show mercy."

"How can you be sure?" she whispered.

Hank leaned forward. "I've seen his kind before, Emily. And I know you have, too. In a man with less control over his demons, he's the kind who'd cut a whore to pieces just to watch her bleed. And who'd stick up for a dead whore? No one. No one except you and me."

Mistress sucked in a deep breath as she dropped her hands into her lap. For a long moment, neither of them said anything.

Then, finally, she spoke. "He's never been here. Never set foot inside the doors. If he goes some place, it's not here. Nor is it anyplace within a two-day ride. I have connections, you see. I've been trying to find something on him, as well. To no avail."

"Ah." Hank suspected as much, but he'd been hoping that Mistress would have something he could use.

"There was a day, several months ago—it was right before the first time you came to visit Miss Green—that Mayor Dupree was late. Which was unlike him," she added weakly with a faint smile.

Hank was pretty sure he knew what day she was talking about—it was most likely the day that he had first kissed Raymond. They had lingered in the office. "Go on."

"I received a note." Her voice was shaking, Hank realized. "It requested Miss Green. I still have it." She rose and moved to a cabinet at the side of the room. After several moments of looking, she pulled out a thin sheet of paper. "It's unsigned but I knew who it was from. I've seen his handwriting on arrest warrants before, but he could always claim his assistant wrote it. There's nothing we can trace back to him."

Hank took the note from her and held it up to his nose. He inhaled deeply—yes, that was the paper smell that had been on Hobson's person. Hank would never forget it. Then he read the note.

Mistress—I request the honor of Miss Green's presence in my chambers immediately for an interrogation.

An interrogation? So that's what they were calling it these days. Hank shook his head and handed the note back. "It's him, all right. But I don't think it's anything we could hold over him. It sounds more like an arrest warrant than anything else."

"Yes, I thought so, too." She put the note back in the case and shut the drawer. "Just to be clear, I am not adverse to sadism. I have one girl here who would welcome the chance for such an 'interrogation' and she commands top dollar for her services, as well as a girl who would thrill at the chance to conduct such a conversation. But Miss Green is not one of those girls and the note…" Her voice trailed off as she looked at the cabinet, worry obvious on her face.

"Miss *McCartney* would be terrified," Hank agreed. "Given her history."

Mistress rolled her eyes, the most undignified thing he'd seen her do yet. "Is there anything you don't know?"

"Hobson. But otherwise, no. I make it my business to be well informed. Knowledge, as I'm sure you know, is its own power."

Mistress ran a manicured fingernail on the desktop. "That is all I can give you."

"By itself, the note won't accomplish much. It's unsigned and the language is too broad. Could you send your girl to him?"

Mistress shook her head. "For that type of play, I will not allow my girls to leave this establishment. There is safety in numbers and I will not send anyone alone to his chambers, no matter how badly we might need information. The risk is too great that he would go too far and I wouldn't be able to live with myself if that happened. My first duty is to the girls still under my protection. I'm all they have, you understand."

She was telling the truth. She really did care about her girls. Hank had been on his own for so long that the concept was something he was still struggling to get his head around. "You are the very finest of mistresses," he told her sincerely.

An almost innocent blush came to her cheeks. "Thank you, Mr. O'Shea." She paused, as if considering her next words carefully. "There is one other person who might have more insight into this... issue than we have."

Hank cocked his head. "Aye?"

She wasn't looking at him. "If someone needed to escape from a man—or a woman," she added with sadness, "and just disappear..."

He understood immediately. "Free Franklin."

"Indeed."

Of course. Free Cyrus Franklin was a black man who lived miles outside of town. There were rumors that he helped slaves—former slaves, now—journey west with new names, new references and a surprising amount of new money. "If Hobson used someone hard, they'd hide."

"They'd run to ground." She sighed. "I've had two girls disappear on me and I suspect Franklin had a hand in helping them out. Which," she added, a quiet fury in her voice, "was unnecessary. If the girls wanted to leave, I wouldn't have kept them here."

Hank debated the veracity of that statement and decided to let it slide. Perhaps it was true—Mistress had, after all, let Emmy go. But maybe the other girls hadn't felt they had as much of a choice.

"I'll ask around," Hank promised. He stood to go.

"Mr. O'Shea?"

He turned back. "Yes?"

"Should I have a... *problem* that I can't solve on my own, may I come to you for assistance?" She looked up at him through her lashes. "There is only so much that a woman in this world can accomplish."

"Are you offering to put yourself in my debt? Because my first duty is always going to be to Mayor Dupree and his betrothed, Miss McCartney. *Always.*" But that was a risk in and of itself. As long as Emmy was merely his betrothed, the risk would be even greater.

Mistress gave him a long look but Hank didn't even bother to blush. She could infer whatever she liked from that statement. "I would have it no other way. No, what I'm offering is an exchange. I'll see if I can find out anything else about Hobson and, in return, should I one day need a problem solved, I will call upon you." She lifted a gentle shoulder. "It seems fair to me."

"Aye," he agreed. He didn't necessarily want to

put himself in Mistress's debt—but then again, their interests were allied on this.

He turned to go again, but again she stopped him. "Mr. O'Shea?"

He paused with his hand on the doorknob. "Yes, Mistress?"

She wasn't looking at him. She was studying something on the desk. "Emmy needs the protection of his name. As long as she is alone, neither you nor I can protect her from Hobson. It can't wait until after the election. Respectability can come later."

"Yes, Mistress."

Funny. Hank had been thinking the same thing.

Chapter Fourteen

W hat do you think of this?" Emmy held up the two sheets of fine paper for Mrs. Logan. She'd rather have asked anyone else to help her pick out her personal stationary—even Hank, for pity's sake—but Mrs. Logan was completely respectable and the two of them shopping for the things Emmy would need as a proper married lady was an acceptable social outing.

"The pale cream sheet," said Snyder, the dry-goods shopkeeper, "is made in New Orleans—I fear it would be too common for you. Now, that pale pink comes all the way from Nice, France," he added, mispronouncing the city's name so it rhymed with *ice*. "Quite a lovely paper, that. Perfect for a fine lady such as yourself."

The man just barely managed to refrain from winking at her and Emmy just barely refrained from rolling her eyes at him. He'd paid for her time often enough once his store had become more successful. Not that his wife knew that—the poor woman was on her eighth child and obviously couldn't keep track of all those children *and* her husband.

No doubt Snyder was hoping Emmy would take the French paper—it was bound to cost three times what the American paper did. She turned to look at Mrs. Logan. "Well?"

"He's left out the most salient point," Mrs. Logan sniffed as she glanced toward the jar of peppermint sticks on the counter.

Emmy smiled. "I'll take the cream—and two peppermint sticks, please." Mrs. Logan could use a little more sweetness in her life.

They finished up their shopping and headed toward Howard Orillston's shop to see if the man could produce the new parlor furniture Emmy required. While Raymond's parlor was in fine repair, it had not been updated since his mother had last done it, nearly ten years ago. Emmy had decided that freshening up the room in a tasteful, understated way would be another good way to show her newly respectable tastes.

Plus, hiring a local woodworker to build the furniture instead of ordering it from out of town was a signal that Raymond was committed to this town.

Then they would be off to the milliners and after that the bakers. Then they had to head back to Mrs. Logan's house, where Ebony White would slip quietly in through the back door for another fitting of Emmy's dress. Raymond and Hank had wanted Emmy to break from the Jeweled Ladies completely—but Emmy would go mad without *someone* to talk to.

Besides, Ebony could sew the most amazing creations and even though the gowns were considerably more modest, Emmy still *felt* like herself. Plus, it was a gift to have someone besides Mrs. Logan to talk to. Ebony kept Emmy up on all the latest gossip—but more than that, they talked of the future. Emmy wondered if she'd be good enough for Raymond, and Ebony shared that she wanted to open her own shop and she hoped Emmy didn't mind, but if anyone asked where she got her gowns, if she'd send them to Ebony?

Those afternoons—those were the moments when Emmy no longer felt like Emerald Green. Instead, she would get a new dress fitted and look at herself in the mirror and see Mrs. Raymond Dupree looking back at her.

This was possible. And, what's more than that, it was *happening*.

There was so much to do to plan for a wedding of this magnitude, it seemed—and Emmy was beyond overwhelmed. Hank and Raymond had decided that the wedding needed to be moved up to next month—a mere four weeks away. Emmy wasn't exactly clear on why because she was just sure that they had all agreed it would be best to wait until *after* the mayoral election instead of just before it.

She had the distinct feeling that both men were holding out on her—but she had no opportunity to press them for more information. In the few moments she had alone with Raymond, he danced around her questions with a politician's skill and Hank simply ignored her questions in their letters.

All Raymond would say was that waiting any longer seemed pointless and besides—wasn't she excited about getting out of Mrs. Logan's house and back to him and Hank? And Emmy was, but...

But something else was going on and it did not bode well that they had apparently decided she couldn't know about it. When she got those two alone again, she was going to give them a piece of her mind.

"I'm sure that pink paper cost a fortune," Mrs. Logan said around her peppermint stick.

"Then I made the right choice, didn't I? I don't want to be seen as unnecessarily extravagant. Imagine how Mayor Dupree's opponents could twist something as simple as a stationary purchase around."

Mrs. Logan nodded in agreement. "Oh, yes—the mayor's fancy wife insists on French stationary."

Emmy giggled—was that how people were referring to her? *Fancy*? That beat being called a sluttish whore, but it was still a ways from proper or respectable, that was for sure.

The schoolmarm, Miss Krenshaw, walked past them just as Emmy laughed. "Miss Krenshaw," Emmy tried to school her features into a more serious, respectable look—but she failed, if Miss Krenshaw's stiff, "*hmph*!" was any indication.

Emmy tried again, aiming for a more polite tone. "Do the new readers for the children meet with your approval?"

"They are acceptable, although tainted by your sins," Miss Krenshaw sniffed. "I do wonder if it would have been better to do without rather than accept books purchased with ill-gotten gains."

Emmy stiffened. This was not how things were supposed to go. She was supposed to spread some money around Brimstone in a philanthropic way and the townspeople were supposed to be grateful and accepting. "Mayor Dupree contributed the funds," she lied.

"And we all know how keen his judgment is," Miss Krenshaw sniffed, her eyes blazing behind her tiny wire spectacles. Before Emmy could reply to that pointed barb, the schoolmarm stalked past, her shabby dress billowing out behind her.

159

"Well," Mrs. Logan said. "That was unpleasant. Never you mind, dear," she said when she saw the look on Emmy's face. "Spinsters like her are crabby for a reason. They are jealous."

Emmy doubted that, but she accepted Mrs. Logan's words of comfort and they continued on their way. She and Mrs. Logan hadn't made it a half block to the woodworker's shop when a voice behind them called out, "Miss... McCartney, is it now? A moment of your time, if you please."

Emmy turned—and froze. Because standing directly behind her at a distance of no more than three feet was none other than Judge Gerard Hobson.

"Land's sakes!" Mrs. Logan squawked in alarm. "Where the devil did you come from?"

There was a hardness to Judge Hobson's smile that physically repelled Emmy a step back. She didn't like being this close to him. She knew the judge didn't like Raymond—and was, once again, running against him for the mayor's office.

But there was something about the man... It was his eyes—narrow and cruel.

She recognized something in his eyes—something that overrode her years of training to say and do whatever it took to please and handle a man. Because she'd seen that look before. The way Judge Hobson was looking at her now was the same way the man who'd tied and horse whipped her a decade ago had looked at her.

He wasn't the same man. Emmy knew that. The man who'd beaten her mercilessly had been shorter with a wider chest and missing a tooth, the money he'd promised to pay Emmy most likely stolen. Hobson was pale and taller, more refined and elegant. But the hardness—that was the same.

It terrified her.

Unconsciously, she stepped in closer to Mrs. Logan. Emmy knew how to defend herself and she also knew that it was unkind to expect Mrs. Logan to put up a fight on her behalf. But she couldn't quite control her reaction to this man. "Your Honor—it's an..." she swallowed, all of her manners deserting her in her time of need. "An honor," she finished, holding a hand over her throat as if she could protect the sensitive skin from him.

He bowed in acknowledgement. "A word, Miss McCartney?" He motioned toward the confectioner's shop.

"I cannot possibly allow Miss McCartney out of my sight," Mrs. Logan spoke up. Her voice was at least three times as shrill as Emmy had ever heard it. Mrs. Logan put a hand on Emmy's arm, as if she wasn't going to allow Judge Hobson even the possibility of pulling Emmy to the side.

God bless her, Emmy thought. She was going to buy Mrs. Logan all the peppermint sticks the older woman could eat. Maybe even a new dress.

"It isn't proper," Mrs. Logan finished. "Say what you have to say, sir."

Judge Hobson favored Mrs. Logan with a hard glare, but the older woman refused to back down. A lifetime of peppermint sticks for that woman, Emmy decided.

"Very well. How fortunate you have someone so concerned with your reputation," he said in an icy voice, turning his full attention back to Emmy. "For a price, I'm sure."

She must have tensed because Mrs. Logan squeezed her arm. "I am lucky to have many people who are concerned with my well-being and salvation, your honor," she said. Somehow, she'd managed to sound pleasant instead of terrified. It was a small victory, but she'd take it.

His eyes glittered with... satisfaction? How could that answer please him? "I'm delighted to hear it, Miss McCartney. I only wished to give you my congratulations on your upcoming nuptials in person. I'm so very pleased you're marrying our illustrious mayor—and what's this I hear about the wedding being moved up a whole month?" He chuckled, a mirthless sound, as his gaze traveled over her muslin day dress. "He can't wait, can he? Or is it you who can't wait?"

Emmy drew as much strength from Mrs. Logan as she possibly could because there was nothing good about amusing—or pleasing—Judge Hobson. "Yes, well, Mrs. Logan has been assisting me in planning for the event and we do have a schedule to maintain. I thank you for your kind thoughts and will be sure to pass them on to Raymond." She gave her smile her best effort and then turned to go.

"What are you going to give him? As a wedding present?"

She turned back, steeling herself for those eyes again. "I'd prefer not to say," she said, trying to sound light. "I wouldn't want you to ruin the surprise, Judge Hobson."

His laughter that time felt more honest—and all the more terrifying for it. She tried to back up another step, but Mrs. Logan held fast.

162

"My dear lady," he said with the faintest hint of a sneer in his voice, "you are a delight. I'm so very glad he's marrying you. You'll completely destroy his career and his reputation and he'll smile as it all crumbles around him." He reached out and touched a finger underneath her chin. "I couldn't have planned it better myself."

She couldn't help it—she flinched. And damn him, his eyes darkened with what was an unmistakable rush of pleasure. She knew all the signs too well.

He wanted her afraid and cowering. So had that other man, the one who'd nearly killed her. Her fear was the seduction.

And Hobson couldn't have it. He couldn't have *her*—not now, not ever. The anger caught and burned and she welcomed it. She jerked her chin away from his touch and turned to Mrs. Logan. "I suddenly find the air here is quite bitter smelling. Shall we?"

The older woman gave a swift nod and, arm in arm, the two women walked away from the odious man. "What a bastard," Mrs. Logan said under her breath once they had safely crossed the street—and confirmed that Judge Hobson was still on his side. "I've never liked that man and if I could, I wouldn't vote for him."

Emmy tried to breathe regularly but it wasn't going well. "You don't think…"

"What?" Mrs. Logan prodded after a long pause.

That he was right. That Emmy would not only cost Raymond this election, but his career. His very reputation. She was trying so hard—so *very* hard—to be a respectable woman worthy of Raymond's love. She had moved in with Mrs. Logan and agreed to all sorts of restrictions on her behavior to prove that she was good enough for Raymond.

No, it was more than that. She had to be worth saving. Because that's how Raymond was framing this—he loved her and was saving her from the sexual drudgery of the Jeweled Ladies.

True, that was not the real reason, not for any of it. Raymond needed a wife to cover up his affair of the heart—and the body—with Hank. And Hank had promised that he could keep Emmy satisfied. The marriage was just a front for something far more scandalous.

But it would all fall apart if Raymond actually married her and lost because of her, wouldn't it? He would be out of a job and, if that happened, Hank would also be out. She knew Raymond had money left over from the Dupree fortune his father had built, but this wasn't about the money. Not really.

Raymond loved politics. He did good things for his constituents. And Hank... well, Hank enjoyed pulling the strings and raising his station. Raymond was the public face and Hank worked behind the scenes. They were perfectly matched and if all of that crumbled because of her...

They'd hate her. Oh, maybe that was a little too dramatic—but they'd resent her, all the same. And resentment bred hate.

What she and Raymond had—beyond an appreciation for Hank O'Shea's more physical attributes—was a delicate bond over his secret. A secret that Emmy had protected for months—and would continue to protect at all costs.

But if he married her...

It would be a lifetime of men like Mr. Snyder at the dry-goods store making obvious innuendos because Emerald Green had spread her legs for him. Of Judge Hobson using her past as a blunt weapon against Raymond. Of respectable people like Miss Krenshaw seeing nothing in her but a sinner putting on airs.

Judge Hobson was right. She would cost Raymond his career.

She couldn't do that to him—to him or Hank.

"Miss McCartney?" Mrs. Logan said, her voice brimming with worry. "Are you well?"

"I'm... fine," she said. "That man just rattled me."

"He can't touch you like that," Mrs. Logan fumed, all but hauling Emmy toward the woodworker's shop. "I won't allow it. You're a respectable woman, for God's sake."

But she wasn't. And as long as she was in Brimstone, she wouldn't be.

She had to leave before she ruined them all.

"Mrs. Logan," she said, trying to keep her voice from catching, "I need to make an additional stop."

"Oh?" The older woman studied her closely.

"Yes," Emmy said, fixing a placid smile to her face. This was the only way, she realized. Why hadn't she seen that earlier? "I need to visit the bank."

Chapter Fifteen

Raymond, get up." Hank shook him roughly, forcing Raymond out of a deep, blissful sleep. Sated and happy, he slept better with Hank beside him.

"What's the matter?" he asked, sleepily reaching for his lover. And then he heard it—the pounding.

"Someone's here. Get dressed." With that, Hank was out of the room, almost as if he'd never been there to begin with.

Raymond tried to get his mind functioning again—the pounding wasn't helping. It couldn't be good. It was the insistent pounding of disaster, rather than the gentle knocking of a social call. What time was it? He got a lamp lit and looked at the clock over the mantle—three a.m.

Finally, his senses came into focus and he threw himself out of bed. He and Hank had taken to sleeping nude—it made everything *so* much easier—but he had a dressing gown and a loose fitting pair of pants of soft flannel. He threw on both things as quickly as he could and, taking the lamp in hand, headed downstairs.

By the time he got halfway down the stairs, the pounding had stopped. His lamp threw the shadows onto Hank—wearing an unbuttoned shirt and trousers with the suspenders hanging down—standing in front of...

"Mrs. Logan?" The older woman turned a worried face to him and, for the first time, Raymond began to panic. "What's wrong? Where's Emmy?" Because what else could have her here at this time of night?"

"She's gone. I'm so sorry, Mayor—I had no idea that she was even thinking of leaving. Everything seemed fine..." Mrs. Logan sounded like she was on the verge of tears.

"Let's go to the parlor," Hank said in a surprisingly soothing voice. "And start from the beginning. Tell us again what happened."

Raymond felt exposed standing here in his dressing gown with Hank in a state of undress. It wouldn't take much for Mrs. Logan to put one and one together and come up with two.

Luckily—or perhaps unluckily—the woman was too overwrought to make a connection. "I had to get up," she said in a frantic voice. "I'm an old woman and I went out to use the privy—I usually do, once a night..." Her cheeks scorched red to admit to this basic fact in front of two young men.

Hank patted her hand as he sat her down on the settee. "Perfectly understandable. What happened when you got up?"

"There was this note..." Mrs. Logan held out a small sheet of paper folded in half.

Raymond stepped forward to take the note. He opened it and read, *"It's all become clear now. I can't do this to Raymond. I love him too much to ruin him."* That was painful enough to read. But it was what came after that felt like a knife slipped between Raymond's ribs. For Emmy had signed it *"E. Green."*

Emerald Green.

167

Raymond handed the note to Hank, trying to get his brain to work. Why would she do this? They had a plan. They needed her—he needed her. And Hank wanted her and so… why would she run?

He must've said the words out loud—hopefully not all of them—because Hank said, "I don't know. But I aim to find out. Mrs. Logan, tell me everything that happened yesterday with Emmy—I mean Miss McCartney."

Mrs. Logan still looked stunned—she'd obviously missed Hank's slip of the tongue. "Everything was normal, until we went to do our shopping."

"Where did you go?" Hank asked patiently, but Raymond wasn't feeling patient anymore.

Emmy was gone and they needed to find her and bring her back. If she didn't want to get married, that was one thing—he wouldn't force her to do anything she didn't want. But he was certain that she had been excited about getting married—about joining him and Hank. About leaving Emerald Green behind. Why would she go back to that name? Surely she wasn't going back to that life—was she?

"We went to the dry goods store first to select the stationary she would use as Mrs. Dupree." Mrs. Logan was speaking only to Hank, no doubt because Raymond hadn't yet managed to put together a coherent thought. "Mr. Snyder was helpful, but perhaps overly friendly, in his way."

Raymond winced. In other words, Snyder had probably paid for Emerald Green at one point or another. But he hadn't thought that that was the sort of thing that would bother Emmy.

"She bought me a peppermint stick," Mrs. Logan

said with a touch of wonder in her voice. "She really is a delightful girl. So thoughtful."

Not *that* thoughtful, not if she had just up and taken off in the middle of the night.

But Raymond kept his thoughts to himself and Hank asked, "Indeed—and what happened after that?"

Mrs. Logan stared for a moment. "She attempted to speak to the schoolmarm, Miss Krenshaw—but the woman tried to cut her. The ungrateful wretch can't even manage to be thankful for the new readers."

Again, that was an expected response. Disappointing, yes—but not surprising. Miss Krenshaw was known for her strict adherence to morals.

"Go on," Hank said encouragingly.

"And then we met..." Her voice trailed off and she looked horrified.

"Who?" Raymond demanded. "Tell me."

Hank shot him a quelling look, but Mrs. Logan was the one who spoke. "Judge Hobson."

Raymond gasped and Hank, for the first time, looked panicked. "Think carefully, Mrs. Logan," Hank said. There was nothing soothing or gentle in his voice this time. "Tell me exactly what the judge said to you and Miss McCartney."

Mrs. Logan nodded. "He wanted to congratulate her on your upcoming wedding," she said, looking to Raymond. "He wanted to speak to her alone, but I wouldn't allow it. It wasn't proper."

"You did well," Hank said, but Raymond could hear the impatience in his voice.

"He also thanked her. He said that..." She swallowed, and looked regretful. "I didn't think she would take it seriously. He's just a bitter old man,

169

making other people unhappy so that his own unhappiness seems justified."

"Mrs. Logan, what did he say to Emmy?" Raymond demanded, barely managing not to shake her by her shoulders.

"He thanked her," she said in a shaky voice, "for destroying your career. He told her that you were going to lose the election because of her and that he couldn't have planned it better himself. He touched her on the cheek and she flinched and I wanted to hit him, but that wouldn't have been proper either, so we turned to go and he left, and it was—it was awful. Miss McCartney was right to be afraid of him, I fear." Her eyes were wet when she looked up at Raymond again. "You don't think he took her, do you? I'll never forgive myself if he did."

Raymond's stomach turned at the thought and even Hank looked stricken. "She would not go quietly, if he had," Hank said, but Raymond could hear the doubt in his voice. "She would've found a way to wake you up. No," he went on, sounding more confident this time, "I think she was frightened and she ran. She would do anything to keep Mayor Dupree safe."

Raymond and Hank shared a look. Anything— which had, until this very afternoon, included marrying Raymond and keeping Hank on the side.

But Hobson had scared her, badly enough to run away from the two people who would do everything within their power to keep her safe. This was beyond the pale and Hobson was going to *pay*.

Raymond was not a violent man—never had been. He knew that there were times when violence was called for and it was one of the reasons why he had first hired Hank. Brimstone was still a rough town and sometimes force had to be met with force. Just because Raymond didn't have the stomach for it didn't mean he wasn't aware of it.

But for perhaps the first time in his life, he wanted to kill someone. With his bare hands, with a gun, with a knife—it didn't matter. As long as Hobson suffered and suffered mightily for this. It was one thing to try to intimidate Raymond, to run against him. That was politics. Raymond was a man and he could take it.

But Emmy? Oh, Emmy...

It was clear now that he and Hank should have done a better job of explaining the risk Hobson posed. But Hank had said that he would take care of it and Raymond had trusted him.

This was the first time that Hank had let him down and it was an odd feeling. One thing however was very clear—he could not rely on Hank to fix this problem. He needed to get his future wife back.

"Is there anything else you can tell us, Mrs. Logan?" Hank was still being reasonable. Raymond almost laughed at the strangeness of it all. Normally, he was the reasonable one and Hank was a man of action. But all Raymond wanted to do was throw on his pants and boots and find Emmy.

"She went to the bank. She withdrew a large sum of money." Mrs. Logan dropped her head into her hands. "I should've known then. But she said she was going to use it to pay for her wedding gift for the mayor. I should have notified you right then and there..."

Hank stood and helped Mrs. Logan to her feet. "Here's what I need you to do now. Go home and act like nothing is amiss. If anyone calls upon Miss

McCartney, you are to tell them that she has taken to her bed with a headache. No appointments, no wedding plans—she has fallen ill and needs to rest. Can you do that?"

Mrs. Logan nodded. "I won't fail you again."

Hank escorted the woman to the door. Raymond didn't stick around. He was already flying up the stairs, hurrying back to his bedroom and throwing off the dressing gown.

They had to get Emmy back and convince her that she belonged with them. She mattered more than the election, more than the office of Mayor. Raymond felt the fool because of all the things he'd promised her, he still hadn't convinced her of that one simple thing— she was more important than his career. He had left room for a whisper of doubt in her mind and Hobson had taken that doubt and made it a cacophony of noise that drowned out all reason.

"Ready?" Hank said, sticking his head in the room. He, too, had finished dressing—black pants, a black jacket and a red bandanna tied around his neck. He looked like a bandit.

Raymond looked down at his own outfit—if they were going to do something illegal, he probably shouldn't have gone with the gray. But he didn't have time to change again. "Where do we even start? You don't really think Hobson has her, do you?"

Hank shook his head. "He wouldn't dare do anything that stupid. No, he made his play and she fell for it. Dammit, we should have warned her."

"But we didn't and we can't change that now. All we can do now is get her back and make sure she's safe."

Hank nodded in turn. They paused only long enough for Raymond to lock up the house behind him. There was too much risk that Hobson was counting on this and would try to break into the house while they were gone. "We'll need horses quickly. And the story as to why."

"Where are we going?"

Hank looked up at the dark night sky as if he were praying. "We're going to pay a visit to Free Cyrus Franklin."

Chapter Sixteen

Emmy sat at the scarred table in the crowded kitchen and kept her gaze focused on the cup in her hands. The handle of the mug was missing, but the coffee was fresh and hot and she knew that, when she'd finished this, there would be more.

It was safer to look at the coffee than it was to look at the man sitting across from her—even though this was his table and his coffee and he was being generous to share both of them with her.

Free Cyrus Franklin hadn't asked any questions of her, except for the most polite ones. He had asked if she might come in and if she would like some coffee and that was, more or less, the extent of their conversation.

Or it had been. "I must say, it has been a long while since I had such a fine lady stop by for a visit." There was a pause. "At four in the morning." There was a hint of humor at the edge of his voice that shone through the thick southern accent. It sounded familiar, almost.

Her grip tightened on the worn mug. "I'm sorry to disturb you. But..."

"You didn't know where else to go," Franklin finished with a chuckle. "No one who winds up here

ever does. You hungry? I could do with some bacon."
It was only when Franklin stood and turned his back to
the table that Emmy chanced to look around.

The kitchen was small and everything in it was
worn. She'd heard Franklin had money—but she didn't
see any sign of that here. The table was only big
enough for two and it crowded against the far side of
the kitchen. There was barely enough room for the
large stove that Franklin was cooking on.

She studied his back. Franklin was only an inch or
two taller than she was, but compact and, she
suspected, muscled underneath his plain and worn
clothes. His skin was far, far darker than Ebony
White's at the Jeweled Ladies—even darker than the
doorman Samuel's skin. She had no idea how old he
was—he could be thirty or fifty. His wiry black hair
was peppered with white and there were lines around
his eyes and mouth that went with his easy-going
smile.

She had seen Franklin before, of course. He'd
passed on a note about Millie in the dry goods store
that one time. She had been Emerald Green then and
now she...

Now she didn't know who she was. She didn't
want to go back to being Emerald Green, but she
wasn't Emmeline Dupree, either. And Emmeline
McCartney didn't fit her anymore—that was a name
she had outgrown a decade ago.

As Franklin fried the eggs and bacon, she wondered
if she had done the right thing by coming here. Things
were less clear in the morning than they had been last
night, when Mrs. Logan had locked up the house and
gone to bed. Emmy had spent a frantic hour packing as

much as she could, as quietly as she could, before leaving a note she feared was woefully inadequate and stealing the horse from the livery stable.

It'd taken her most of the night to find Franklin's house. There wasn't much west of Brimstone and traveling in the dark on a nearly moonless night was a dangerous proposition at best. She was tired to her bones, sick with worry and more scared than she wanted to be.

"I suppose we should discuss your arrival," Franklin said as the bacon began to sizzle. "You in trouble?"

"I suppose." She swallowed, not ready to discuss anything yet. "Have you heard from Millie?"

"Every so often," he said agreeably, letting the conversation go anywhere but to where he'd suggested. "She's got a little baby girl now. I think they're right happy folk."

She closed her eyes and tried to breathe through the stab of pain that hit her mid-chest. When she and Hank and Raymond had reached their agreement, they'd decided only that the children would carry Raymond's name but be loved by all. Everything else would come later. They had been more concerned about what the children would look like than whether or not she wanted them.

But for the last month and a half, she'd begun to think about it more. She didn't want to have children right away—she wanted to get settled into this new life, her new name. She wanted to become Emmeline Dupree in every way. But one day...

She thought of fat little babies with black hair and bright blue eyes. They had been nothing more than a vague, undefined dream and now they never would be.

"Will anyone be coming after you?" Franklin asked in a soft voice. Emmy started and looked up to see him standing next to her, a plate heaped with eggs and bacon in his hand. "I don't need to know why, but I do need to be prepared."

"I'm not sure. They might not notice I'm missing for hours yet."

Mrs. Logan normally was up by six in the morning. It was still several hours off. She'd have to find the note and then...

And then what? She wouldn't go to Hobson, Emmy felt sure of that. But she might go to Raymond—and Hank.

Surely, they would see the wisdom in this. If Raymond especially could just put his feelings for her aside, he would be sure to understand why she had slipped off into the darkness. It was for his own good, after all. And as for Hank... Well, it wasn't as if they were in love. Hank was good in bed—maybe the best she'd ever had and that was saying something. She would certainly miss *that*, but it wasn't as if she didn't know how to procure sex on her own.

"Will Mistress be coming after you?" Franklin asked as he sat down on the other side of the table, a plate in front of him.

Emmy shook her head. How odd that Franklin would even ask about Mistress. She knew that Mistress was not a huge supporter of Franklin's, but she didn't want to be a source of contention between them. Between anyone, really. But she felt the need to explain. "I just need to go somewhere and start over. Somewhere where no one's ever heard of me."

Franklin tucked into his breakfast as he

177

considered this statement. "Weren't you doing that already? Marrying the mayor and becoming respectable?"

"I was going to cost him the election—his entire career. He shouldn't have tried to lift me up." She swallowed against a lump in her throat. She was irredeemable. "It was a mistake to try."

"Your mayor—he's a good man," Franklin said sympathetically. "There's a lot of them in town that'd like to burn me out, but not him. A man with power who supports a freedman like me—even if it's quietly—that's a rare thing." Emmy didn't have a response for that. "Have you talked to him about this?"

She shook her head, but just then, a man loomed in the darkened doorway of the kitchen. Emmy let out a little squeak of shock but Franklin seemed unconcerned. He looked at the man, who made some sort of gesture with his hands that didn't make any sense to Emmy. Franklin understood, though. "Riders?" The strange man nodded. "How many?"

The man held up two fingers.

Emmy wilted. Two riders at what was fast approaching four thirty in the morning could only mean one thing—Raymond and Hank had come for her. Part of her was thrilled—there was a certain romantic quality to the two men riding hell for leather to save her from an unknown future. But it also meant that they were idiots because they didn't understand. She should've left a longer note—a separate letter for Raymond. She should have done... Something. Anything to make them let her go.

Franklin's gaze cut over to her. "This a problem?"

Emmy did not know if she should laugh or cry or

178

both. "I suspect it's the mayor and his assistant come to fetch me back."

The man in the doorway—little more than a pale shadow—stepped into the room. He was a hulking man, broad and mean looking. And silent. Completely silent. Franklin held up a hand and the man stopped. "Do you want to go back, Miss?" That made Emmy almost smile—Franklin didn't know what to call her either. "If not, we best hide you now. There could be trouble and I hate to see a woman as lovely as you get caught in the cross fire."

"No!" she said, rising to her feet so quickly she almost knocked the chair over. "No—I don't want any gunfire. I don't want anyone to get hurt."

"*Franklin*! Wake up, man—we need to talk to you!"

Franklin and the silent man stared at her. "It's Raymond," she said weakly.

"And it wouldn't do to get into a gunfight with the good mayor," Franklin laughed. But that was cut short by the pounding on the front door of this little house that was barely more than a shack. It rattled the tin plates stacked on a shelf. "Time to make up your mind, Miss. Hide or face what awaits you." More pounding followed.

Emmy couldn't decide. They had come for her— but could she really face them and still leave?

"Franklin," came a different voice—heavy with an Irish accent, "don't make me break this door down."

The silent man fidgeted, but Franklin just waited. "I can protect you, but you have to want to be protected," he said softly.

"Emmeline is missing," Raymond yelled and she

179

could hear the fear and worry in his voice. "We have to find her before Hobson does."

Oh, Lord. Is that what they had convinced themselves was happening?

The silent man stiffened at the mention of the judge's name. Franklin reached out and put a hand on his arm to calm him. "Last chance," he said, with a gentle smile.

"I will... I will speak to them." She didn't really have much of a choice. To run off and leave Raymond—and Hank—with only a note that probably didn't make much sense because she'd been so upset when she'd written it—no wonder Raymond sounded sick with worry. She couldn't do this to them, but she couldn't stay with them, either. She squared her shoulders and, out of habit, shook out her riding skirt.

Franklin nodded to the silent man and he seemed to melt back into the darkened hallway. Franklin stood and grabbed the lamp from the table and motioned for Emmy to follow him. The pounding on the front door was beginning to sound less like knocking and more like someone having a go with a battering ram. Franklin waved Emmy into what passed for the parlor in this house and went to open the door.

She sat on a shabby chair and tried to steel herself for what was about to come. They wanted her back and they were worried about her. But she was worried about them. It was all such a mess in her head.

The door creaked when Franklin opened it and then Raymond and Hank were talking at the same time.

"Is she here? Is she all right?" That was Raymond.

"Start talking." That was Hank, sounding more angry than Emmy had ever heard him sound before.

"Gentlemen," Franklin said with what Emmy was beginning to realize was his usual good nature. "The lady is waiting for you in the parlor." Then he made a *tsking* sound. "Y'all did a number on my door."

"I'll pay for a new one." And then, Raymond was in the parlor, rushing over to where she sat and falling to his knees. "Darling," he said. It wasn't an act. Not any of it. "I've been worried sick about you. Are you all right?" As he spoke, his hands moved over her— her face, her shoulders, her arms and hands, making sure she was whole and unharmed. He settled his hands around her waist and stared up at her. "It's all right," he said in a whisper and it was only then that Emmy realized she was crying.

"Saints be praised," Hank said in a voice that was part whisper, part growl as he came in behind Raymond. Franklin joined them, so Hank stayed on his feet and kept a respectable distance between him and Emmy. When he got a good look at Emmy's face, he fiddled with the cloth around his neck and removed it, handing it to her. It smelled of him and that made her cry all over.

What was wrong with her? She had done worse, survived worse—and she never let her composure slip. As Emerald Green, she had been the greatest actress of her age.

But this wasn't an act and Emerald Green was dead. This was all suddenly more real than she knew how to deal with.

"I'll just get that coffee," Franklin said. "But, gentlemen—if you attempt to remove the lady from

181

this house without her permission, you won't make it back to town." The menace in his voice made Emmy shiver.

"We wouldn't think of doing anything with the lady without her permission," Raymond snapped off impatiently.

Hank just turned to Franklin and gave him a long look before saying, "I'll help you with that coffee."

And that made Emmy cry even harder because if she were going to have a conversation about the rest of her life with these two men, she actually wanted both men to be a part of the conversation. Yet even now, their wickedness had to be hidden. Hank left the room.

"My darling Emmy," Raymond said, pulling her into his arms. Somehow, he wound up sitting in the chair with her curled onto his lap. "Are you all right? I cannot tell you how worried I have been."

"You shouldn't have come," she said, clinging to him even as she knew she shouldn't. "You should let me go."

"Why on earth would I want to do that?"

She forced herself to look up at him. "I'm going to cost you the election—your entire career. No one in town will ever respect you ever again. I'll always be the whore you married."

He kissed her for head. "And you believed Hobson?"

"You weren't there. It's not just Hobson. It's Snyder at the dry goods store and the schoolteacher and the entire *town*. I will always be soiled to them and I will only soil you in turn." She couldn't fight back the tears, so she buried her face in his shoulder again. "I'll ruin you."

Raymond chuckled and she wanted to strike him. "First off, Hobson is not going to win because of you. He's going to lose because of himself. I'm sure the people like the schoolteacher want him to win, but the majority of people in Brimstone don't wish to live their lives according to his desires."

He was making too much sense. She could feel herself starting to waver. "That may have been true before we announced our engagement, but..."

"No *buts* about it," he said more sternly. "I am so sorry, my darling Emmy."

If she had hoped that things would start making more sense now, she was sadly mistaken. "Why are you apologizing to *me*?"

He cupped her cheek in his palm and tilted her face so that she had no choice but to look him in the eye. "Because I asked you to marry me without making something explicitly clear—that you are worth more than my career."

Her cheeks warmed. "But I'm not. And you're only marrying me because of..." Because of Hank. Because Emmy understood Raymond's need for that man and no other woman would.

He touched his lips to hers—a chaste kiss that did little to warm her. But it did make her feel better, in its own fashion. "Emmy, I love you. I wouldn't marry you if I didn't. Yes, there are advantages to the match for both of us—at least I hope you consider the advantages to you—but I do love you. Just..."

She smiled even as she sniffed. "Just not like that. I adore you as well. But I'm nothing but a whore. And I don't want you to resent me. Because you will, if your career crumbles because of me."

He studied her with a half smile on his face, his arms strong around her. "Do you know what I want?"

"Hank," she whispered, ducking her head again.

He chuckled. "I want to do some good in this world, Emmy. I have ideas. Like streetlamps. We could install gas streetlamps in Brimstone and make the streets safer after dark."

She stared at him incredulously. "Streetlamps?"

"It's just an example," he said, stroking her cheek. "But that's what I want—I want to make things better and leave my mark on this world. Sometimes it'll be messy and sometimes I'll lose. You can't take responsibility for my career."

"You're trying to change my mind," she murmured.

"Is it working?"

She nuzzled back into him. "And what of Hank?"

"We should have done a better job explaining how Hobson might have twisted the truth." Raymond sighed. "He tried to buy Hank away from me and he's tried to intimidate me in much the same way he did you. But we didn't think he'd make such a play with you."

Emmy gasped. "He *what*?"

"He's focused and dangerous. My darling, did you stop to think how it would look if you disappeared?" When she didn't have an answer for that, he said, "I didn't think so. I've publically professed my love for you. I've helped you leave your life of sin behind. I'm going to marry you. There will be those who never approve, but if you stood me up at the altar and disappeared, do you know what people would say about that?"

Shame burned at her cheeks and her neck. "I didn't think…"

"At the very best, my already questionable judgment would be even more in doubt because I gave my heart to a woman who couldn't be true. But I have no doubts that rumors would swirl that I had a hand in your disappearance. Hobson would fan those flames until I was little more than a man who murdered his whore bride and buried the body."

She couldn't help the shudder than ran through her body. "Oh, Raymond—I'm so sorry."

"If you don't want to marry me, then I will release you from the agreement." His voice was stiff and she knew that he didn't want that to happen. "You are free to do what you want and I never want you to feel trapped or compelled against your will. If you really want to go away and start over, I'll make sure you have the funds you need to live comfortably."

"I have my own money," she said, patting the belt underneath her riding dress.

He sighed. "All I would say is that, if you want to leave, you let Hank and I arrange it for you. No more slipping off in to the night, courting danger and scandal. I couldn't bear it if something happened to you."

"Do you really mean it?"

"Oh, Emmy." He curled his arms around her and pulled her in closer. If only they were in a bed in their nightclothes, the covers pulled up over them. "You have saved me. If I hadn't found you, I... I don't know if I'd still be here. I was so alone in the world before you and you gave me the faith to hold on for Hank. I want you to stay but more than that, I want you to be happy. That's all I've ever wanted for you."

She began to cry again in earnest. "But what of Hank?" she sniffled. "I wish he were in here with us."

185

He kissed her forehead again. "We are united on this, darling. He wants you and he considers you a trusted friend."

"I don't love him." It felt like a betrayal to admit it.

"You don't have to. Right now, all anyone is asking of you concerning Hank is that you trust him. Trust that he has your best interests at heart. Trust that he can satisfy your every craven desire. Trust that he will make you happy. If you can be friends with him, love might come later."

He had convinced her, damn it. "I failed you. I didn't trust you."

"No, darling." He kissed her again. "You didn't trust yourself."

And the fact that he was right had her weeping all over again.

"Come home with me," he whispered as he comforted her. "With us. We'll go to my house and you can spend the day in bed."

"With you? Both of you?"

He stilled underneath her. "We only want to take care of you. However you want, we'll be there for you. For always, Emmy. You don't have to face this life alone."

The words were like a balm on her soul. She had made a mess of this—of being an honorable, respectable woman and yet, Raymond still wanted her. Hank still wanted her. They wanted to take care of her and make her a part of their lives.

"Be our family, Emmy," he pleaded.

How could she say no to that? She couldn't. So she kissed him, long and slow and, yes, with heat dancing at the edge of their lips. "Take me home, Raymond."

Chapter Seventeen

Hank stood in the ramshackle kitchen, watching Free Cyrus Franklin put on more water for coffee. It was killing him to stand here instead of flying back to the parlor and taking them both away from this house.

But Raymond was the one who persuaded people to do things. He'd convince her. Hank had faith in his man. And, as much as he wanted to make sure Emmy was all right, he couldn't waste this opportunity.

"Heard of you," Franklin said as he ground the coffee beans. "The mayor's right-hand man. O'Shea, right?"

"Aye." He needed to ask Franklin about Hobson, but that was the sort of thing a man had to lead up to.

"The Irish bastard?" It could have been an insult from anyone else, but Franklin had an easy humor about him.

"Been called worse," Hank agreed, letting a smile play on his lips. "This isn't what I expected," he said, changing the subject.

"It isn't?"

"We heard you had money and places to hide people." He didn't see either of those things here.

Franklin snorted. "I don't take you as a man who

187

believes everything you hear, O'Shea. Or see. I'd have thought a man like you would have made a visit before now, get the lay of the land—that sort of thing." He paused. "Guess you always had somewhere else to be."

"Aye," Hank said, deciding that small talk was better left to Raymond. He jumped into the gap. "Actually, I was speaking about you just the other day."

"Oh? Good things, I hope."

Hank didn't reply.

For the first time, a ripple of tension moved over Franklin's shoulders. "Who?"

"The Mistress of the Jeweled Ladies."

Franklin tensed. "I suppose she asked for you to deliver my head on a platter."

"No. She told me to ask you for help."

It took a moment for this to sink in. Franklin shook his head and then cracked a huge grin. "That woman never ceases to amaze me."

Did Franklin know Mistress? "She's a piece of work, she is. But we have a mutual problem and we hit a dead end."

"What?"

"Hobson."

The effect of these words was immediate. Franklin groaned and slumped into one of the mismatched chairs at the table.

This noise brought a ghost into the kitchen. Hank jumped and, acting on instinct swung at the huge white man who appeared out of nowhere.

"It's okay," Franklin said as the ghost stepped clear of Hank's fist, leaving him embarrassingly off balance. "Isaac is my extra set of eyes and ears. For now, anyway."

188

Hank stared between the two men. "Where the hell did he come from? This place isn't that big."

"Isn't it?" Franklin chuckled. "It's okay, Isaac. Discussing our mutual acquaintance, Hobson."

Isaac took another step into the room, which pretty much filled the rest of the small space. He made a strange grunting noise but didn't say anything else.

"What do you want with Hobson?" Franklin translated.

"He's a risk to us."

"And Mistress?"

There was a tenderness in Franklin's voice that surprised Hank. "Aye, to her, too. And you. He'll come for all of us because we won't bend to his will."

Isaac made another distressed noise. Hank notched an eyebrow at the giant—he would not be caught off guard again.

"And how do I figure into this?" Franklin spoke with caution now.

"I can't find a thing on the man to hold him in check. I went to Mistress because she and I have an... understanding, if you will, and I was hopeful that maybe she'd have a different knowledge of him than I do. But she didn't have anything that we could use."

"You want to blackmail the man?"

Hank let that question hang in the air for a moment. He could hear a low murmuring coming from the front of the house—Raymond and Emmy.

Please let Raymond be convincing her.

"How did you think Mistress would help you?" The man's easy-going nature was gone now, which meant Hank had to be getting close.

Closer, anyway. "I know Hobson's type. I thought

189

maybe he'd have a girl that he went too far with, cut her up and left her for dead, maybe. But Mistress said the man's never crossed her threshold and none of the other madams would admit to anything."

"Too scared," Franklin agreed. Isaac made some sort of motion with his hands and Franklin nodded. "I can't help you."

Damn. "On principle or because you don't have anything?"

Franklin snorted. "I'll be honest, O'Shea—I like your mayor. He leaves me be and I get the sense that he deflects attention from me whenever people get it into their heads to get riled up. I know that if Hobson ousts the man, I'll be in trouble and I'm not of the mind to be starting over. Again."

"Aye." He wasn't of a mind to start over, either—and, if Raymond could just convince Emmy to come back to them, he wouldn't have to.

But that still left Hobson. "I can tell you what I know but it won't do you any good. I don't keep written records. On principle," he added.

Hank sighed. He couldn't be surprised by that—but it was disappointing. "What?"

"Had a girl come through—oh, probably four years ago. Before your time, I reckon. A whore—but not one of Mistress's. She keeps too good an eye on her own, that one."

Hank fought the urge to shake the man. He didn't need asides—he needed information. "And?"

"She was from several towns north. Someone dumped her on my doorstep in the middle of the night and rode off. She was barely alive when I found her in the morning. Lost a lot of blood, a lot of broken bones."

So it was as Hank had thought. Hobson was barely in control and if that control slipped, he could kill a person. "Did she make it?"

The giant Isaac made another inhuman noise and left the room as silently as he'd appeared in it. "No," Franklin said sadly. "She didn't. And I can't even prove that what she whispered as she lay dying was 'the judge.' Just that it sounded like that."

"What's with your man?" Hank asked, nodding toward the door where Isaac had disappeared.

"He came looking for her. Hasn't spoken in four years. Not sure he's ever spoken. Sharp, though. He stayed. Nowhere else to go without the girl."

Damn it all to hell. "I needed something to use, Franklin. Something concrete."

Isaac reappeared. How the hell could a man that big be that quiet? He looked at Franklin and the black man nodded.

Isaac approached Hank and held out a square of muslin that had been tied with a faded orange ribbon. "Open it," Franklin said. "He's the one giving it to you, not me."

Hank took the bundle and undid the tie. Inside was a torn piece of cloth—a necktie, maybe? It had a ragged tear in it. Hank lifted the cloth up and something small tumbled out into his hand.

A pin. A small gold pin.

"That was in her mouth," Franklin explained as Hank studied the pin.

Four years ago. If this was Hobson's work—and the tie could have easily been his, the pin too—then four years ago...

He'd lost the election to Raymond right about

191

then. The upstart Dupree had taken what Hobson considered his by rights and the judge had gone too far in a rage.

"Does he know you have this?"

Franklin shook his head. "No way to prove it's his, either. But it's all Isaac has of Mollie's."

The giant looked stricken. Hank held the bundle out and Isaac took it, disappearing again. "It's not enough. Ties and pins are common."

Franklin shrugged. "I told you. Think your mayor's going to lose?"

"In the grand scheme of things, it doesn't matter. He's going to be moving on from Brimstone sooner or later. The statehouse is calling."

"Someone'll need to stay behind to protect the town."

Hank smirked. In the silence that followed, more murmuring floated up from the front of the house. "Not me. I go where the mayor goes. But you..." he said, nodding toward Franklin.

The man laughed. "I don't think so. I like my life just fine."

Just then a little girl—brown with her hair in braids—stumbled into the room. "Hungrwy," she murmured, ignoring Hank entirely and making straight for Franklin, who pulled her onto his lap.

"Good morning to you, too, Bessie. I thought you remembered the rules?" The little girl stuck her thumb in her mouth and leaned into Franklin's shoulder.

"The rules?" The little girl stared over at Hank, her eyes going wide as she finally registered his presence.

Franklin shot him a grin over the child's head.

192

"When there's people in the house, they're to stay hidden until Isaac or I give the all clear."

Hank just shook his head. "Do I even want to know where you keep them all?"

"Nope." He bussed the top of the child's head. "Your ma is sure gonna be worried about you."

The girl didn't say anything. She just stared at Hank with her thumb in her mouth.

"You didn't see her," Franklin prompted.

"Who?" Hank replied.

"Thanks." Floorboards creaked from somewhere else. "Ah, sounds like they've reached a decision." Isaac reappeared and Franklin handed the child to him. "See her ma isn't worried," Franklin said before leading Hank back down the narrow hall.

No doors, no windows. The house had looked like a shack from the outside. Where the hell was he keeping multiple people?

But before Hank could answer that question, the parlor door opened and Raymond stepped out into the narrow hall—his arm around Emmy's waist and their heads bent together.

Relief bloomed in Hank's chest. God bless Raymond's silver tongue. "Mr. O'Shea," Raymond said, "I believe we best take Miss McCartney home."

"Yes," she said, looking up at Hank with a potent blend of happiness and sadness—and desire. It went straight to his cock, that look did. "Take me home."

"You sure?" Franklin asked. Hank could've kicked him.

"I am." She gave a little curtsy to Franklin. "Again, I'm so sorry to have disturbed you this morning. Thank you for your kindness—I won't forget it."

"My pleasure, Miss."

Raymond guided Emmy out of the house, but Hank held back. "If you find out anything…"

"I'll keep it in mind. Mr. O'Shea?"

"Aye?"

"It was a pleasure." Franklin extended his hand and Hank didn't hesitate.

He gave the man a firm shake. "If you need anything, you know how to find me."

Then he was out the door, mounting up and riding back to town as dawn broke over the horizon.

They were taking Emmy home.

Chapter Eighteen

They made it back to Brimstone just as dawn broke. Raymond carried Emmy into his house while Hank returned the borrowed horses back to the livery stable.

"But I need to get back to Mrs. Logan," she said, exhaustion clawing at her.

Raymond kissed her forehead again as he carried her up the stairs. She wanted to protest, but she couldn't. All she could do was cling to him. "Didn't you know? You've taken ill and are confined to your bed." He made a humming sound. "Or my bed, as the case may be." When she started to protest, he interrupted her. "Emmy, if you think I'm going to shunt you away instead of making sure you're safe and whole and happy, then you've got another think coming."

He carried her into the master bedroom and gently sat her down on the bed. "God, Emmy—you have no idea how frantic with worry we were."

She knew that he wasn't trying to make her feel bad—but it happened anyway. "I'm sorry." She was so tired that she was on the verge of laughing and crying all at once.

She was not, by rule, a hysterical woman. She had faced life with her head up and her shoulders back—

her father's death, followed by her mother's decline and passing. The realization that the only way that a gently bred young woman such as herself, alone in this world, would ever be able to step outside of the bounds that society had set for her was to flip up her skirts and pretend she enjoyed it. Even being savagely beaten— she braved that pain until she had passed out.

But this was different. Because, aside from the passing of her parents, all of those other things had seemed to happen to someone else—Emerald Green. They were borne out of necessity. She had always managed to keep a stone wall between what her heart wanted and what her head knew it had to do to survive.

"I love you so much, Raymond." Because that stone wall? It didn't exist anymore. "I never meant to hurt you—or worry you."

Gently, he pulled her to her feet and began their old ritual of undressing her. He unbuttoned her riding habit and then carefully folded it and laid it over the back of the chair so it wouldn't wrinkle. Which was, in light of everything that happened, rather humorous. She's ridden God-only-knew how many miles across the Texas plains under cover of darkness—the riding habit was beyond wrinkled. She smiled.

And when she started to smile, she started to giggle. Once she started to giggle, she couldn't stop. Raymond unlaced her stays and set them to the side. Normally, this would be as far as he went. She was down to her shift and stockings—but he didn't stop. Not today.

Instead, he stripped her down to her bare skin and then sat her back on the bed. He went to the nearby washstand and came back with a damp cloth, wiping

196

away the grime from the ride and the tears that had muddied together on her cheeks. Slowly, with great care, he stroked the cloth over her skin and the giggles died away.

"This feels lovely," she told him as the tension of the last day melted away under his touch.

He rinsed out the cloth and came back to the bed again, kneeling before her as he stroked the cloth over her breasts and her stomach. "I think I would be a terrible husband," he admitted as she leaned back on her elbows while he continued to work the cloth lower over her body.

"How so?" Her breath caught in her throat as the cloth dipped in between her legs and stroked along her thighs.

"I should've done this for you already." His voice took on a new tone, huskier than she'd ever heard it before. "I always believed that there was nothing in this for me—and maybe that's still true for every other woman in the world—but you're different, Emmy. And I have not paid enough attention."

He pressed a kiss at the top of one of her thighs and then sat back as he ran the cloth over her legs.

"I never asked you to. I know this is not what you dream of at night." But even as she said it, she could feel other parts of her body beginning to tighten up as the months of celibacy began to catch up with her.

"But if I'm to be your husband, I should take care of you. In my own fashion, of course." He stood and her gaze dropped to his pants. She was nude and spread out before him, beginning to ache with the need. And even though his voice had deepened and his eyes had darkened and he had touched her in places

197

that he had never touched her before, she could tell at a glance that he still wouldn't be able to take her.

She sat back up and began to unbutton his shirt for him. "You give me so much and yet you worry that you're not giving me enough." He shrugged out of the shirt as she unfastened his trousers.

"I don't worry," he corrected. "I know. Because if I had given you what you needed from the first, you wouldn't have run. The next time you get scared," he told her as he kicked out of his trousers she began to undo the drawstring of his drawers—something she had never done before either, "be honest. Tell me what the problem is and let me help before you make a rash decision. But I failed as well because I hadn't warned you like I should have. I have to make you feel secure in your place by my side and in my bed."

And then he was before her. She leaned her head against his waist and studied him—touched him, even. He didn't shrink away from her as her fingers stroked over his rod. He was neither fully limp nor hardened. "This fits you," she said, tracing his outline. She so rarely got to see a man when he wasn't hard that it was novel to study her future husband in this way. He was rather longer than most men, but not quite as wide—certainly far more narrow than Hank was. The hair at the base of his rod was neat without being unruly and he hung almost completely straight. "Perfect," she decided.

"Come to bed, my love."

They slipped under the covers, arms around each other. Raymond kissed her slowly as he worked the remaining pins free from her hair. The sweetness of it made Emmy ache all the more.

She had no idea how long they lay there, whispering sweet nothings in each other's ears and kissing and touching—but never going any farther than that. Then, suddenly, something in the air changed and she knew without even looking that Hank had arrived.

"That may be the prettiest picture I've ever seen," came his deep voice from the doorway.

Raymond just smiled down at her. "Would you like Hank to join us?" He asked it in a loud enough voice that it carried to where Hank was standing. "I know you wished he could have been in the parlor with us at Franklin's house. Let us take care of you, Emmy."

She nodded and leaned up enough that she could see Hank, still some ten feet away from them. "Come to bed, Hank. I've missed you."

"And I, you." Emmy lay back on the soft pillows and let Raymond kiss her as she listened to the sound of Hank shedding his clothes. He splashed in the wash water and then, to her surprise, he slid into bed next to her, instead of behind Raymond. "Sweetling, I'm so glad to see you."

Because she and Raymond were tangled up so closely together, she felt his arousal immediately. But before she could tease him, Hank pressed against her, his mouth consuming hers. All of the heat that was missing from the way Raymond touched her caught and burned bright because now Hank was here and they were both going to take care of her.

"May I kiss you still, darling?" Raymond asked and she could hear his excitement in his voice.

She broke away from Hank and turned back to Raymond. They had her surrounded in the middle of the great bed—big enough for the three of them. "Please do." She slid one hand around the back of Raymond's neck and pulled him down to her lips. With the other, she buried her fingers into Hank's hair.

Hank needed no such encouragement. He trailed kisses down her neck and then latched on to her breast while Raymond kept possession of her mouth. There, Hank suckled her as his fingers moved lower and stroked at her pussy. "Aye, you have missed me, haven't you?" he asked, his accent stronger as his fingers dipped into her.

She moaned against Raymond's mouth. "Yes." But that was all she was able to say because Hank was scraping his teeth along her nipple, adding pressure as he sucked. But the thing that had her breathing hardest was the fact that Raymond joined in. He squeezed her other breast and ran his fingers around her nipple. It was not an expert gesture—but it excited her all the same.

"Is that all right?" Raymond asked with such innocence that it made her want to laugh. And she did.

"Wonderful," she told him. Then she pulled on Hank's hair and dragged him back up to her mouth. Their tongues tangled as he added another finger and began to stroke her with a maddening rhythm.

For years, Emmy had engaged in bed play multiple times a night. She'd had so much sex and so many different kinds of sex that it all ran together.

But this? After two long months of being touched by no hand but her own, this stood out as something wild and beautiful. Raymond kissed at her neck and made it as far as the tops of her breasts while Hank worked her body with an almost savage fury. She

200

could feel both of their rods bumping against her hips, but they made no move toward each other. Instead, they dedicated their attention to her.

She broke quickly under Hank's skilled touch, but instead of relieving the ache deep inside of her, it only made it worse. "I need more," she begged shamelessly. She had never begged before. "Please, please give me more."

Hank rolled her away from him so that she was facing Raymond. Then he lifted her leg and slung it back over his, opening her for him. "And I will always give it to you, sweetling," he said, his voice close to her ear. He positioned his thick rod against her and sank in with one thrust.

Emmy cried out with relief as he filled her—it had been so long. "I missed you," she said over her shoulder.

"And I, you. Raymond," Hank added, "give me your hand."

Raymond did as he asked and Emmy held still, waiting to see what wickedness Hank had in mind for the three of them. Hank guided Raymond's hand, starting high at Emmy's breast and stroking Raymond's fingertips over her stiff nipples. But neither lingered. Hank continued to guide Raymond's hand down over the swell of Emmys stomach and then lower, between her legs. "Spread your fingers—aye, that's it." And then Raymond's hand was against her sex, his heel pressing against her, his fingers on either side of where Hank was lodged deep in Emmy. "When I thrust into her, you'll feel me move through your fingers."

Emmy exhaled heavily as Hank let go and brought his own hands back up to her breast. "Oh, Raymond—Hank—that feels good." She forced her eyes open and studied Raymond. He had never touched her so intimately. "Are you all right?"

His eyes had gotten wide again—innocence still dancing at the edges. "He feels so thick in you."

"Aye, and I'll feel just as thick in you when it's your turn. But you had me last night and Emmy needs me more." Slowly—tortuously—he began to move in and out of her, setting a languorous pace to give Raymond a chance to adjust to this new joining, no doubt.

Emmy moaned as Hank fucked into her and tormented her nipples. He was right—she needed him *so* badly right now.

"What should I do?" Raymond asked, sounding a little nervous about the whole situation.

"Hang on." Hank paused and shifted, tucking his other hand underneath Emmy and cupping her breast with that one. Then he reached around front and took hold of Raymond's rod. "Move your hand back and forth—yes, like that. I can feel you and you're hitting her where she needs it most—isn't he, Emmy?"

"Oh, God, yes," she moaned as the heel of Raymond's hand pressed her sex.

"And kiss her, if you want." Hank began to move again.

Emmy couldn't keep her eyes open as the sensations flooded over her. "Or kiss him, if you want."

"Oh—*oh*." Raymond's voice was tight with tension. "In other words, I should kiss someone?"

Emmy didn't get the chance to say *yes* because his lips crushed against hers. For the first time in all of her time in bed with Raymond, there was true heat behind his lips, no doubt because Hank had taken him firmly in hand.

Raymond pulled away from her and leaned across her body so that he could kiss Hank. Emmy watched, trying to focus. It seemed so right, the way their two mouths met and broke apart and met again as Hank fucked her and stroked him.

Raymond turned his attention back to her. "Is this all right?"

She was past words now, being carried away by the relentless pressure of Hank burying himself inside of her again and again, of Hank tweaking her nipples and biting the back of her neck—and Raymond rubbing against her sex and pressing against her pussy where Hank slid into her.

She didn't try to fight it, didn't try to hold off. She let the wantonness of these two men taking care of her sweep her away until waves of pleasure broke over her and she shattered like she had never shattered before. She surrendered to it, knowing that she was safe and secure and *loved*.

"So beautiful," Raymond ground out through gritted teeth and then he exploded against her stomach.

Hank was the last to come and he pulled out to do it. As he spurted against her backside, Emmy was only dimly aware that he must not have rolled on the rubber. Even in the throes of passion, he still remembered and honored her wishes.

They lay together, a tangle of arms and legs and wetness and happiness, until Raymond finally pulled himself away. "I believe we made a right mess of the bed, as you would say," he said, smiling at Hank. He went back to the washstand and wet the much-used cloth again.

He cleaned Emmy's front and Hank cleaned her

back and then Raymond climbed back into bed where they all curled around each other. "I love you," Emmy murmured into Raymond's hair as the exhaustion caught up with her.

"And I, you," Hank whispered against her ear.

"Will you stay?" Raymond cupped her face and kissed her cheek.

"I don't think I could go anywhere if I wanted to," she responded with a sleepy smile. "I heard I was sick and needed to stay in bed all day."

Hanks fingers danced over her ribs—light, but teasing—and Raymond just smiled at her. "I mean, will you marry me and stay with us? Will you trust us when we both tell you that you are more important than my career? Will you let us make you happy?"

It wasn't fair, his question—she was sleepy and completely sated and would have happily agreed to almost anything he'd asked of her. But this was what she had to look forward to for the rest of her life. It wasn't all just for Raymond. She wouldn't be his wife solely to make him happy or further his career. It would work both ways now, she realized. She would make him happy and he would take care of her. He would be able to touch her and hold her and maintain the closeness that she had come to prize over their months together and with the addition of Hank, she and Raymond would be able to love each other as they had never been able to before.

And she would be able to love Hank. How could she not? She knew now what she hadn't the first two times she had met him—that he had been making sure she was a good fit for Raymond—not his career, but a good fit for the man. But they'd moved past that now—now Hank was proving that he was good for *her*. And he was.

"Well?" Hank asked as he kissed her neck. "Will you have me? Will you let me into your marriage bed?"

She rolled onto her back and pulled both men so that they rested against each of her shoulders. Sometimes, Hank would be in the middle and sometimes it would be Raymond. But no matter what happened, it would be the three of them.

She kissed Raymond and then Hank in turn. "I wouldn't have either of you any other way."

Grinning, Raymond brushed a lock of hair away from her forehead. "I can't wait to marry you, darling."

Married. She would be a respectable woman at last.

Then Hank moved against her and Raymond's gaze sharpened and her lust rose up again.

Well, she thought with a smile as she succumbed to passion yet again. Maybe not *that* respectable.

Epilogue

In the end, no one gave Emmy away. She gave herself away and she did so with a smile.

Although it was highly irregular, Mrs. Logan acted as her matron of honor, and of course, Hank stood with Raymond. No one else knew that there was a third ring in Hank's pocket, one that would not be used during the ceremony. But when Raymond and Emmy said their vows, Hank would slip his ring on his finger, too, on the right hand instead of the left, so as not to draw attention.

It was the most wonderful day of Hank's life.

The inside of the Methodist Church was beautiful, Hank thought with a sigh. The afternoon light hit the stained-glass windows and bathed the entire crowd in pink and blue light. A great many of Brimstone's finer families showed up to see the spectacle of the mayor marrying a whore. The fact that they were willing to watch this ceremony unfold—and, by their mere presence, give their tacit approval—boded well for Raymond's reelection chances. A few of the Jewels had shown up as well, but their dresses were surprisingly demure, compared to what they normally wore.

Mrs. Logan managed not to scowl her way down the aisle, which was impressive, given the woman's occasional sour disposition. Then the organ music swelled and Emmy appeared at the end of the church, resplendent in a white gown with lace that buttoned up to her neck and came down to her fingertips. Miss White had worked day and night to get it ready on time, but it was worth it. Her hair had been swept up into a tasteful twist on the top of her head and, aside from a veil of delicate lace, her only decoration was a pair of pearl studs in her ears.

But that was all the decoration she needed. She was simply the most beautiful woman that Hank had ever seen and after this, she would be theirs. Oh, yes, officially, she would be Raymond's, but they knew the truth and that was the important thing, wasn't it?

The crowd stood as she proceeded down the aisle. The pews were packed, but a quick glance told Hank that no one had made it up to the dark balcony. Then, some movement upstairs caught his eye and he looked again.

A face—almost as dark as the darkness itself—leaned forward. Hank recognized him—it was Free Cyrus Franklin, come to watch a happy ending in action. Hank gave a little tilt of his head in the man's direction and was rewarded when he got one in return. But then something else up in the balcony shifted, drawing the attention of both men.

Hank had the sense that the second figure was a woman, but that was all he could tell. The figure came to sit near Franklin, and the man pulled back into the shadows.

Hank smiled. No one else knew the two were up there, silent witnesses to this most unusual wedding.

Emmy glided down the aisle, perfectly radiant in the happiness. "She looks stunning," Raymond whispered to Hank.

"Aye, beautiful," Hank agreed.

This was a new phase of his life and for the first time, he felt unsure about his footing. Raymond and Emmy were suddenly his family. Lovers and companions and friends, all at the same time. It was perhaps more than he'd ever thought he'd achieve—and certainly more than he ever thought he might deserve. Becoming Hank O'Shea had been the first step on a journey that had led him here, standing next to the man he loved and waiting for the woman he adored.

His work wasn't done. Brimstone still had rough edges and every day, more people arrived—former slaves, veterans of the war, people looking for a fresh start. Raymond still had an election to win and, from there, a political career to build. There would be setbacks and struggles—there always were. But for the first time, Hank wouldn't be facing those alone.

As she reached the altar, he caught Emmy's eye and smiled, a small, private smile just for the two of them.

This was, officially, the end of Henry Moynihan. Although Hank had put that troubled boy aside years ago, he had hung on, lingering in the background, ready to do what he had to in order to survive again. Pick up, leave town, start over—anyway he could, he would've.

But, as Raymond and Emmy exchanged vows before the preacher, the crowd and God himself, Hank knew that Henry was never coming back. He was Hank O'Shea. He belonged to Raymond and Emmeline Dupree. He had a home now and roots— roots that would grow into a tree. Children, maybe.

He glanced around the crowded church again. Judge Gerard Hobson wasn't here. For the best, really.

Because God help that man if he came for Hank's own ever again.

About the Author

Thanks so much for reading this *Jeweled Ladies* story! Leaving an honest review or telling a friend what you thought is the best way to show the love for your friendly local author!

Who is Maggie Chase? Writer, reader, crafter—I've told a lot of different stories a lot of different ways as Sarah M. Anderson, but the Jeweled Ladies series marks my first foray into historical erotica. I passionately believe that every single person deserves their own happily-ever-after and my stories reflect that hope on the page.

Readers can find out more about Maggie any of the following ways:

Sign up for her newsletter:
http://bit.ly/maggiechasenews

Visit her website:
http://www.maggiechase.com

Check out her Tumblr:
http://themaggiechase.tumblr.com/

Follow on Twitter:
http://twitter.com/TheMaggieChase

Leave a review on Goodreads:
http://www.goodreads.com/maggie_chase

Get Amazon pre-order information:
www.amazon.com/author/maggiechase

Other Books by Maggie Chase

The Jeweled Ladies: The Mistress Series

His Topaz
Their Emerald
Her Ebony
His Sapphire
His Crown Jewel

The Jeweled Ladies: The Rogues Series

His Diamond
Their Amethyst

Now Available from Maggie Chase

Ebony White needs to learn to read and the prickly schoolmarm, Minerva Krenshaw, needs a new dress. But when Ebony strips Minerva bare, will the temptation overwhelm them both?

Read on for an excerpt of
Her Ebony
a Jeweled Ladies story

Minerva absolutely needed to move. To move *away*, she quickly corrected. She needed to stand and put some distance between her and her student.

"I couldn't help but notice," Abigail said as she tugged the strings of Minerva's bonnet loose, "that you added some lace."

Minerva could feel her sweet breath bouncing off of her skin. She needed to put space between them. But she couldn't. "It made sense, what you said last time. To dress respectably is to be thought respectable."

Move, she ordered herself. *Move.* And it did seem like movement happened. But she would swear that she got closer to Abigail—not farther away.

Oh, it wasn't fair, how pretty she was when her

211

lips curved like that. Minerva realized that she was physically shaking from the effort of keeping her hands to herself.

"Shall I take your measurements now, Minerva?" Abigail whispered softly.

Minerva barely heard her for the pounding in her ears. "Promise you will make me respectable? I mean," she quickly corrected, "make me *look* respectable?" Because she was already respectable. Respectable and honorable and... and...

All thoughts let her mind as Abigail reached over and plucked the top button of her dress, the one right under her chin. "Would it be all right," she asked in that same soft voice that had Minerva leaning forward to catch her words, "if I asked you to step out of this dress?"

"Why?" Panic rose up in the back of her throat like the taste of blood.

"This is how you get a dress made for you." Then, mercifully, Abigail stood. "If I don't take your measurements, it won't fit properly."

Minerva knew that. She had gone with her mother to a dress shop in Albany on more than one occasion. She had just been hoping to avoid it *now*.

She opened her mouth to say as much but then made the mistake of looking up at Abigail's face. The young woman stood before her, her hands clasped almost primly in front of her. But that wasn't what stopped Minerva. It was the look on Abigail's face— the same look that Minerva had only caught a glimpse of through the dry-goods store window.

It was almost as if she could see more to Minerva. Honestly, she didn't know if it was a good thing or not.

"It will be perfectly proper," Abigail added, worry taking hold around her eyes. "I would prefer not to do this in the church… But besides that, there is nothing improper about this at all."

Lies, all of it. Well, except for that bit about doing in the church. But what were the alternatives? She could go back to the Jeweled Ladies and strip down for this woman? Or bring her back to the schoolhouse and disrobe for her there? The only other possible option was to take a room at the Golden Star hotel.

All three involved her and Abigail alone in a room with a bed and very little clothing separating them.

As immoral as it was, the church was by far the safest option.

But she had to try just one more time. "Are you sure this is necessary?"

Abigail smiled and then did the worst thing in the world she could have done—she reached down and took Minerva's hands in hers, pulling her to her feet. "But of course," she murmured. "Would you like me to undo the buttons for you?"

Don't miss
HER EBONY
By Maggie Chase
© 2017 by Maggie Chase
Sign up for the Newsletter
Check out www.maggiechase.com
for more great Jeweled Ladies stories!

www.ingramcontent.com/pod-product-compliance
Lightning Source LLC
Chambersburg PA
CBHW031427200626
46814CB00016B/2495